The MIDNIGHT EXAMINER

THE MIDNIGHT EXAMINER

WILLIAM KOTZWINKLE

HOUGHTON MIFFLIN / SEYMOUR LAWRENCE

BOSTON · 1989

For information about permission to reproduce selections
from this book, write to Permissions, Houghton Mifflin
Company, 2 Park Street, Boston, Massachusetts 02108.

Library of Congress Cataloging-in-Publication Data

Kotzwinkle, William.
The midnight examiner / William Kotzwinkle.
p.   cm.
ISBN 0-395-49859-7
I. Title.
PS3561.085M5   1989   88-38409
813'.54—dc19   CIP

Printed in the United States of America

P 10 9 8 7 6 5 4 3 2 1

The MIDNIGHT EXAMINER

I entered the front door of Chameleon Publications. Hyacinth, the receptionist, was applying plasters to her corns. "Letter from that lawyer for you, Howard."

I glanced at it quickly, saw we were being sued for a million dollars, and walked on, to my cubicle.

My office faced the Manhattan Time Clock Company, its huge wall advertisement faded, peeling; through its windows I could see a gnomelike man at his bench repairing time. Below us was the Sixth Avenue flower district. A light rain was falling on the plants that lined the sidewalks, their leaves and buds uplifted to receive all the poisonous elements in the periodic table. I inhaled a deep draught of toxins cooled by the morning mist and turned to my desk.

Strewn around it were photographs of naked women, as Chameleon Publications included among its periodicals *Knockers* and *Bottoms.* Each of the naked women on my desk had a bikini halter airbrushed across her breasts and a brief bikini panty airbrushed across her pubic region, an expert touch added by Fernando of our art department.

I had purchased the photographs from Herr von Germersheim, a German art dealer who regularly visited our office with a suitcaseful of nude studies. After purchase, Chameleon Publications would then add underwear to the young ladies. Why? Our publisher believed that in the new climate of fundamentalist repression, *Playboy, Penthouse, Hustler,* and all other full-nude magazines would finally be swept from the stands, while ours would remain, girls prancing about in discreet little painted bikinis. "We'll be there when the tide turns," he'd said to me, with an innate capacity for wrong ideas so acute as to approach genius.

A long rectangular plaque on my desk bore my name, HOWARD HALLIDAY, lest I forget it amidst the many identities I assumed from week to week; since, as an economy measure, we never purchased outside material from anyone, our small staff had to write everything, and we all had many names, sometimes we even had the same names, but lately we'd tried to coordinate. I'd assigned each of us one letter of the alphabet from which to choose our noms de plume, and so far this month I'd been Howard Haggerd Halberd Hammertoe Harm Habana Hades Halston Handy Harley Harmon Heman Hence Hardman Hardon.

I drank my morning coffee and ate my breakfast roll, while gazing dully at my desk. The painted women gazed back at me. Many of them I knew personally. Sometimes they borrowed money from me, but more often I borrowed from them, as they were better paid than I.

Upon the wall of my cubicle hung other photographs, of atrocities, anomalies of birth both human and animal, and other bits and pieces of life that come an editor's way, and which he uses when and where he can to add dimension to his publications. Photographers frequently risked their life to get such shots, and I, in turn, paid them as little as I could.

After finishing my coffee, I swallowed some caffeine tablets and began my daily perusal of Miss Agnes T. Wimple's *Study of Grammar*, circa 1924. With it, I was able to diagram any complicated sentences I wrote for our magazines. Each sentence was, therefore, grammatically perfect, a touch I don't believe the readers of *Knockers* often noticed.

There was a knock on my cubicle door and Fernando entered with a new layout. "Here you go, kid, all ready for you to put some words."

A naked female, modestly airbrushed but provocatively poised on the seat of a ten-speed bicycle, was before me. Beneath each photo of the cyclist Fernando had drawn blank lines, the length and number of which determined how much copy I would have to write about the joys of nude cycling. This would then, in part, comprise the text of *Bottoms* magazine, under the guidance of Miss Agnes T. Wimple, deceased.

"I'm tired, kid," said Fernando, sitting down in my guest chair.

"Why, what have you been doing?"

"Workin' on my portafolio. I'm goin' to get a good job with a real magazine."

"*Bottoms* is a real magazine, Fernando." I chewed a peppermint caffeine tablet.

"Chit."

"Chit?"

"Chit." He gestured toward the seminaked cyclist. "All chit." He indicated, as well, other layouts on my desk, to which I had already written a number of lighthearted captions for the discerning reader.

The wall behind my chair gave a sudden thud. This meant that our publisher, Nathan Feingold, was practicing with his blowgun. He'd received it from one of the advertisers in our *Macho Man* magazine, so popular with mercenary groups. Under the nom de plume of Howard Hachett, I piloted *Macho Man* to completion each month, and was in direct correspondence with any number of snake-eaters, one of whom had sent me a crossbow pistol in case I ever had to "kill somebody quietly," not something I thought likely, which shows how much I knew, but this comes later in my story.

Fernando gazed toward the wall, where the darts were still landing with little thuds.

"Please don't think of leaving us, Fernando. We need you." How could I tell him that *Mademoiselle* and *Esquire* and *Vogue* and *The New Yorker* had little use for a man whose job experience had been, to date, painting brassieres on nipples?

"When my portafolio done, I kiss this place goodbye."

Another thud. At times I worried, unnecessarily I'm sure, that a poisoned dart would come through the wall and lodge in my brain. Fernando left the cubicle, and I resumed my meditations, as the office slowly came to life. In the cubicle next to mine the editor of our lucrative weekly, the *Midnight Examiner*, was sorting out pictures of movie stars and athletes, as well as the human interest file of photos of touchingly heroic idiots and four-year-old mothers, people rescued by their pets, the usual hermaphrodite, and a man who had an eel living in his intestines. All of the stories in the *Midnight Examiner* were the brain children of this editor, Hip O'Hopp, an aging newspaper man whom I'd never seen sober. He looked up at me over the partition separating our cubicles. "Can you do a story for me about a woman who gives birth to puppies?"

"When do you need it?"

"By five."

I made a notation on my pad, *woman — birth — puppies,* and placed it beside the other things that needed doing today: As Dr. Howard Husbands, M.D., I had to write my medical column for *Ladies Own Monthly,* our women's magazine, found in more modular homes and trailer parks than any other publication. After Husbands's little number, I had to incarnate as Dr. Doris and bang out my sex and psychology column, always bearing in mind that national surveys had shown readers of *Ladies Own Monthly* were conservative on matters relating to sex, fashion, food, politics, and child care. I looked at a recent letter from one of our readers:

Dear Dr. Doris,

I have a suggestion for parents who are troubled by their children telling lies. Our Bobby was a terrible liar until we hit on the following. After catching him in a lie, we dressed him up in his sister's dress and made him stand in the front yard in it all afternoon.

Enclosed was a photo of Bobby in the dress, looking psychologically scarred for life. The letter concludes:

Now whenever we think he might be getting ready to tell a lie we just say, "Remember your sister's dress."

Seems like a perfectly sensible solution to me. But in spite of such close reader contact, I did not really know the reader of *Ladies Own Monthly*, my picture of her being that of a woman in a Lovable bra who ensures bathroom daintiness with frilly toilet-paper cozies, keeps her soap pads in ceramic animals with gaping mouths, and expresses her inner nature on pillows bearing quaint sayings such as World's Greatest Mom.

I left my cubicle to have a brief morning chat with Hattie Flyer, editor of our popular *Young Nurse Romance, My Confession,* and the occasional one-shot special such as *Brides Tell All*. "Hattie, good morning."

"I had one hell of a night with that friend of yours." Hattie looked as I'd always imagined Agnes T. Wimple must have — slender, myopic, round-shouldered and with a slight crouch to her, as if folded around a secret held tightly in her midsection, the secret of grammar or the secret of — love? On Hattie's computer screen at this early hour already danced a scene of throbbing passion, about people like the friend I'd introduced her to last night, who would be brought low in the end by a plucky heroine.

"How was your reader response this month?"

"Look at it." She indicated a huge pile of correspondence — all of it in answer to a story she'd dreamed up, of a woman whose husband had been rendered blind, deaf, and impotent owing to an unusual reaction to a swine flu vaccination. Hattie had put it directly to her readers. What would *they* do? "Most of them would leave him." She riffled the edges of the correspondence. "They want a new start."

"And we'll give it to them, Hattie."

"We'll give them what we always give them," said Hattie, and indeed this was true. Month after month Hattie would crank out the same old story, her readers would experience the same titillation, hope, inhibition, and resolution, and our publisher would deposit their money in his same bank.

Hattie peered into her screen. Her frizzy carrot-colored hair, which she'd ruined through the use of a home permanent kit advertised in our *Beauty Secrets* magazine, was in a wild halo around her head, the extension of a brain overloaded with impassioned scenarios of lovers hopelessly knotted and intertwined. Her fingers began clicking on her keyboard once more. Her glasses slipped down her little snub nose and she poked them back impatiently, as she bent still closer to her screen; her tiny breasts rose and fell more rapidly as her breath quickened. She crossed and uncrossed her legs, swung one of them rapidly back and forth. Decorum bade me turn away and leave her to her demon lover.

I was met by the sight of Siggy Blomberg, our advertising manager — short, stocky, hurrying toward me, his hands clutching space ads, his face filled with worry, for the products advertised in our magazines came from companies that changed their addresses frequently. In Siggy's hands at any one moment could be found space ads for bed-wetting tablets, pile ointment, and a twenty-four-karat gold-plated Holy Miracle Cross.

"Bust Creme . . ." Siggy shook an ad in my face.

"Hasn't paid up?"

"It turned a woman's ta-tas green. Nathan said I should have product-tested before running the ad." Siggy crumpled up the ad in his fist. "If I product-tested all this crap, I'd have six-inch hairs growing out of my nose."

"We advertise an inexpensive battery-powered rotary nose hair remover."

"Nathan's never met our advertisers. He doesn't know what I have to go through to find these people. Look at this one. *Nu-Age Egyptian Wrinkle Remover. The secret of Cleopatra's beauty. Age-old secret discovered in excavated tomb by noted French scientist, Dr. Louis LaForge.* It's made in a garage in Newark by a coupla ex-cons. You think I'm gonna rub this on my face?"

"Have a peppermint." I handed him one of my caffeine tablets.

He chewed it quickly, swallowed, and shuffled through his other ads. "The strapless brassiere people are reliable. And the vaginal suppositories. But these other momsers . . ."

"Have another peppermint, Siggy. You've got to relax."

"Look at this one. Fellowship Prayer Study Group, The Secret of Christian Morality. They've been screwing me for the last six months. I ask for a check and they send me a pink crucifix."

Hattie looked up from her keyboard. "Do I give this young woman an unattractive squint, or just an all-around inferiority complex?"

"How about a nice little mustache?" Siggy extracted an ad. "I can get her a buy on depilatory cream."

"I'll give her a squint," said Hattie. "And a lovely body, which is unnoticeable because of it."

"A squint down to her knees?" Siggy took another caffeine

mint from my outstretched palm. "The kid's in trouble."

"*He* finally notices how pretty she is, as if waking from a dream, but it's going to be too late for the bastard. He had his chance."

Hattie pushed her glasses back up on her nose with a quick thrust, and resumed clicking. Recognizing the approach of the primal scene, I drew Siggy away.

"How does she write that shit?" he asked.

"She's made remarkable discoveries."

"Ever think of planking her? Well, I've gotta go deal with Nathan over this green ta-ta cream." Siggy started to leave, was stopped by the sound of a dart thudding softly into the other side of my office wall. He blinked nervously. "I never go in when he's got that friggin' blowgun out." Siggy rubbed his hands together, interlocked his fingers, cracked all his knuckles. "Christ, I'm cranked up this morning. It just came over me all of a sudden, I feel like I could jump over a building." He turned toward the door, ads bulging out his back pocket. "I'm gonna go out and collect money from a lot of cheap bastards and if they try to get away I'll kill them."

I watched him hurry off in his ill-fitting brightly polished suit, then turned back toward my own cubicle. Nude cycling doesn't happen by itself, and I had twelve lines to fill. Almost any gibberish would suffice, for national surveys had shown that the average reader of *Bottoms* was a moron.

My intercom buzzed. I picked it up and heard the voice of my publisher.

"*Howard, come in here.*"

I hung up, swiveled toward my wall and listened for the thud of a poisoned dart. Silence. I walked through the edi-

torial office, and out into the hall, where Hyacinth was watering our vast array of potted palms, jades, azaleas, and Japanese bamboo, her dark brown figure framed among them,
young and twiggy, in a white dress splashed with daisies,
looking like the vernal spirit of the flower district.

"Don't open that door till I get outta range," she said, and
put down her watering can.

I waited until she was back at her switchboard, then tapped
on Nathan's door. A grunt from the other side was my signal
to enter, and I did, cautiously.

Nathan sat at his desk — a large kidney-shaped piece of
plastic in which his face was faintly reflected, like a jinn who
counseled him from beneath the waters of a dark pool. He
was a pudgy little man of immense vitality, his eyes red from
squinting along the sights of his blowgun. "Sit down, Howard." He motioned me into a nearby chair, then turned and
pivoted in his own chair toward the window. He gazed outward thoughtfully. "Religion, Howard, we haven't tapped it."

He expected no response. His fingers were drumming on
his little paunch. "I woke up in the middle of the night last
night, I sat straight up in bed and said, *I see the light*." He
swiveled back toward me. "We're starting a new magazine.
Would you mind standin' over there against the wall? I want
to outline you with darts."

"Outline yourself with darts."

"Don't worry, you know they don't go in very deep."

"It's not the depth I'm concerned with, Nathan, it's the
crap you put on the end of them."

"Prophecy."

"Prophecy?"

"*Prophecy* magazine will have full-page ads every month

for Bibles that glow in the dark. Creep along the wall, How-ard, imitating a large ape." Nathan reached for his blowpipe, inserted a dart. I edged toward the door. A hissing dart lodged itself in his bulletin board, next to my right ear. His face flushed from hyperventilation. "How'd you like to become an ordained minister?"

"How'd you like to put that blowgun away?"

"Three bucks is all it takes. The Christian Mail Order Church of California." He inserted another dart in his blow-gun and sent it winging toward me like an angry wasp. It stuck, deeply, a few inches from my left ear. "Front page in color. Use our stock photographs, whatever's in the house, and slap stories around them."

"Tits and ass?"

"With a spiritual twist."

"I Was A Hooker Until I Met Jesus?"

"That's the kind of thing."

"We'll have to hire another staff writer."

"So hire."

"We can ordain him while we're at it."

"Make him a bishop. It only costs ten bucks more."

"I see the light." With my eyes fixed on my publisher's blowgun, I backed out of the office. Our beauty editor, Am-ber Adams, was coming down the hall, looking very tired. "My apartment was robbed last night, and the thief shit in the middle of my rug."

"Burglars frequently do it. It has something to do with their guilt."

"Fuck their guilt."

I'd been in love with her since I'd hired her three years ago. "While events are still fresh in your memory, Amber, could I ask you to write up the account in your own words, giving vent to all your emotion, because I have a hole in this month's issue of *Real Detective,* and a personal narrative like this would fill it perfectly. Call it something like What The Thief Did To Me In My Deepest Privacy."

Nathan's door opened and he stepped into the hall beside us. "You telling Amber about *Prophecy?*"

"A burglar crapped on my rug." Amber angrily stirred her coffee.

"Get a tear-gas gun. Gas him before he squats. *Real Detective* advertises one for twenty-nine ninety-five. Tell Amber about *Prophecy,* Howard. Bring her up to date on Christian beauty care. There should be an angle there." He fixed Amber with his beady gaze. "What do you think of Everlasting Life Collagen and Placenta Gell?"

"It sucks."

"I'm getting the sense of it, Howard. Tap the source. Do you know how much water they sell at Lourdes every year?"

"Nathan, the last time we developed a product and labeled it ourselves — remember? The Male Hormone Spray?"

"I'm going to bring a specialist in on this."

"Not your brother, please."

"Melvin is a brainstormer, Howard. He and I can bat this around and come up with something."

"The last thing Melvin came up with was that fourteen-year-old model. If the judge hadn't been from your old neighborhood you'd be in jail on a morals charge."

"I didn't have a vision then, Howard. I didn't have religion behind me."

"I like Melvin, Nathan. His Male Hormone Spray might have caught on if it hadn't exploded prematurely."

Nathan took me confidentially by the sleeve. He stood just shoulder-high to me and his blue eyes were innocent as a child's. "I have to employ Melvin. He's our mother's sole support. Now — call the employment agency. Get us that new writer. I'm going to the bank." Nathan continued on out of our offices and into the hall, on his way to borrow money for our new spiritual adventure. I slipped another caffeine mint in my mouth and stopped by the desk of Celia Lyndhurst, a young woman who had sensitivity, beauty, style, and who, as editor of *Real Detective* spent her day inventing stories of rape, mayhem, and murder in every possible shade of brutality and grotesqueness.

"Good morning, Celia. Why do you have a pair of rubber flippers under your desk?"

She tucked a strand of waist-length brown hair back over her ear. "I'm studying scuba diving. I'm going to have a murder take place that way, the husband sets the whole thing up, tells his wife they should go to Jamaica together but first they've got to learn how to snorkel, then he kills her in two feet of water." When she smiled, her eyelids elongated and closed up slightly, making her look somewhat sinister, like one of her own ax murderers. She'd graduated from Vassar with a degree in journalism, and had the energy of a wind-up mouse, scurrying in and out of the cupboards of her thought. Smiling, eyes elongating, the dragon mistress of crime spun back toward her computer, and I returned to my cubicle, where I called the Perfection Placement Agency, and was put through to the headhunter I liked dealing with.

"Hello, this is Howard Hammertoe-Halliday at Chameleon Publications."

"I gotta guy here with lots of class."

"Writing experience?"

"He looks like the Duke of Argyle."

"I asked, does he have any writing experience?"

"He's got a hell of a tailor."

"Send him over." I hung up, and went on to my sex column for *Ladies Own Monthly.* Opening a reader's envelope at random I found this question:

> Dear Dr. Doris,
>
> *I been noticing lately that every time I go into the bathroom to bathe, there's a rustling noise outside the window. Tonight I went to close the curtains and caught sight of my own husband out there. He's been hiding in the bushes peeking in at me. What should I do?*
>
> In Despair

> Dear In Despair,
>
> *While other sex therapists might suggest counseling for you and your husband, I suggest moving your bathroom to the second floor . . .*

An hour passed. So engrossed was I in Dr. Doris's frank responses, that it came as something of a shock when Hyacinth announced over the intercom that there was a gentleman named Forrest Crumpacker to see me, sent by Perfection Placement.

"Send him in."

"He's a sharp-lookin' dude. He could teach you a lot."

"I'm open to suggestion."

"You dress like my Uncle Valvin."

"Is there something objectionable in Uncle Valvin's attire?"

"His clothes fit exactly like yours. Look at the back of your jacket, Howard. Collar gaps out a mile."

"I'm right now throwing my jacket out the window, along with my pants."

"An' the knot in your tie's too big."

"I'm tearing it apart . . . just a moment . . ."

"You check this guy out."

Hyacinth hung up. I straightened my desk in preparation for this Crumpacker fellow, and peeked between a pair of *Knockers* which hung on the glass wall of my cubicle. I noted that no artificial fibers clung to his form, that his jacket was a light gray tropical worsted without the offensive gap, his shirt oxford cloth button-down, his tie a dark regimental stripe with small knot. Magnificently creased and tailored trousers completed the outfit. Forrest Crumpacker's attire was the equivalent of a perfect sentence by Agnes T. Wimple.

"Mr. Crumpacker, come in. I'm Howard Hardon-Halliday, editor in chief."

He sat down across from me, his eyes on the pasted-up pages of Nude On A Bicycle. "I saw a man in the hallway with a blowgun in his hands."

"Our publisher. Have you any writing experience?"

His eyebrow was lifted at the photo of a two-headed poodle tacked on my wall. "I write crank letters."

"Any published?"

"Several. In *The Village Voice*."

"Do you know anything about religion?"

"I always give a nickel to the Jehovah's Witnesses when they come to my door."

"Most of your work would be on *Prophecy*. At some point, you may be required to take the cloth."

"Do I get to hear confessions?"

"No, but you may have to write some, as our confessions editor occasionally gets behind with her squalid romances."

"Let me tell you about squalid. I was in a barroom the other night —"

I held up my hand. "Save it, Crumpacker. Don't dilute by premature exposure. Could you do a story about Elvis Presley being alive and well in a convent in Argentina?"

"I think Elvis stood for everything that's fine about America."

We gazed across the desk at each other. The midday light shone through the window onto Crumpacker's sleek black hair. His legs were crossed, one knee swinging with a slight show of apprehensiveness. "Care for a mint, Mr. Crumpacker?"

He wisely declined, his gaze turning toward another photograph on my cubicle wall, of a man having his head ceremonially chopped off in Ghabaghib. "I can't think what I'm doing here, really."

"You're interviewing for a position on a nationally distributed biweekly journal for religious fanatics."

Crumpacker leaned forward, flicked an imaginary speck of dust from the toe of his gleaming shoe. His gaze continued on down the wall of my cubicle to a photograph of Malaysian twins in a bottle; his eyes flicked suspiciously back to mine. Directly behind his head came a soft thump in the wall, of a blow dart sinking into the wood.

"Could you tackle a story about a woman who gives birth to puppies?"

Crumpacker's eyebrow again lifted. "Why stop there? Why not an orangutan? Why not a hippopotamus?"

"Our publisher wants someone who'll be here five years from now."

"Don't be ridiculous." His gaze wandered back to the bottled young Malaysians. "What are they for?"

"Demented Dad Pickles Progeny. Last week's *Midnight Examiner*. Crumpacker, what do you think of my sport jacket? Be honest."

"Well, it has a certain originality."

We turned our gazes to the window. A pigeon had landed on my sill and was coo-cooing. Next door I heard Nathan's window go up. A moment later a dart whizzed past my glass, narrowly missing the bird.

"I think that about concludes our rigorous screening process." I rose and extended my hand. "The position is yours." I escorted him through the office, to the cubicle vacated by our last staff writer after Nathan put a blow dart in his calf. "I need the puppy story by five o'clock."

I saw the cornered look that I've grown to recognize in our writers dawn on his face. "I know you have at least five puppies in you, old man. They don't have to be very big." I left him then, and walked over to Hattie Flyer's desk. She was still hunched over her keyboard, bringing her true life romance to a tearful climax. "There," she said, looking up at me through her fringe of frizzy curls. "He's learned a lesson he'll never forget."

"Brought another arrogant male to his knees, have we?"

"He didn't know what a cute couple they actually were."

"Because of her unfortunate squint?"

"He made her his plaything. He thought that just because he raised thoroughbred horses and lived on a large estate —"

"— she'd be happy to be his slave."

"Now he can go screw his horse." Hattie violently pressed the PRINT button on her computer and a second later, her little printer was zizzing along, giving final shape to another powerful human drama. Continuing my rounds, I found Celia Lyndhurst pulling the switch on the electric chair. A moment later her printer too was zizzing out another instructive human account on the bitter rewards of crime.

In the distance, I heard the wheels of the coffee cart approaching, and I proceeded into the reception area, where I caught sight of Nathan hiding behind the feather plant. "Nathan, come out of there."

He stepped innocently through the foliage, blowpipe in hand. "Is everything on schedule?"

"It's ridiculous for a publisher to be crouching in his own reception area."

"There's nothing like a good ambush, Howard."

"You've been reading too many *Macho Man*s."

"*Macho Man* leads American youth to glory."

"It's only a matter of time before you put another dart in a member of this staff. It creates a mood of fear and uncertainty in the office."

At that moment, Crumpacker entered the reception area. "Who are you?" asked Nathan.

"Nathan," I said, intervening, "this is the new editor of *Prophecy*."

Nathan scrutinized him closely. "You're carrying a great endeavor on your shoulders."

"I've just given birth to puppies."

"Crumpacker, this is your publisher, Nathan Feingold."

Extending his blowgun as if it were a swagger stick, Nathan tapped Crumpacker on the shoulder. "Have you been made a bishop yet?"

"His ordination is being processed," I replied.

"Ask whether we can make him a cardinal. Cardinal Crumpacker has the look we want for the masthead. That's all right with you, isn't it, Crumpacker?" Nathan turned back to me. "I want everybody in the office to do their share for *Prophecy,* Howard. Call a meeting of the entire staff. My office tomorrow morning, ten o'clock. Cardinal Crumpacker will supervise."

We watched our publisher walk off, blowgun cradled in his arms. "A word of advice, Crumpacker. Never enter Nathan's office while he's taking target practice. We don't want anyone else being wounded."

"Anyone *else*?"

"A man named Kloss. Promising editorial material. Felled by a dart in the leg."

Hyacinth nodded her approval as Crumpacker walked past. "Have him take you shopping," she said to me softly.

I proceeded to my cubicle, and found Yvonne Plum waiting for me. Yvonne was the gossip columnist for the *Midnight Examiner* and editor of *Teen Idol* magazine. She gave me a smoldering glance, one eye half hidden by a sweeping wave from her platinum wig. "I've just spent the morning with Duran Duran. They were too much too much. Such impetuous boys."

Yvonne had been one of the first American journalists to interview the Rolling Stones and predicted their career would come to nothing. Now she fanned a handful of Duran Duran glossy photos onto my desk. "They were *very* cooperative cooperative."

I checked my production board. "*Teen Idol* is due at the printer's in two days."

"The printer said there'll be no *Teen Idol* until he gets paid."

"There'll always be a teen idol, Yvonne. Never doubt that."

"Even now they're sewing sequins on his Jockey shorts."

"And even now you're wrapping up the issue that's got to be on my desk tomorrow morning at nine."

"I refuse to be dragged into your compulsive fantasies," she said huffily, then picked up my coffee and Danish and left.

I sat down at my desk and began arranging the pages for *Bottoms*. Each of the seminudes was now accompanied by a suitable text extolling her beauty and the lighthearted lifestyle she enjoyed while walking around in an airbrushed brassiere. I swiveled to my production board and put a check in the Printer Ready column just as my telephone buzzed.

"Howard, come in here, and bring Hip O'Hopp with you."

I walked around my cubicle and into Hip's. He sat before his computer, hammering out the last stories of the week for the *Midnight Examiner*. A medicine bottle filled with gin was close at hand. "Hip, Nathan wants to see us."

Hip sighed, opened his medicine bottle, took a swig. "You have my puppy story?"

"Cardinal Crumpacker is writing it."

Hip nodded, not seeming to know or care who Cardinal Crumpacker was as long as his puppy story was on the way. Hip's personal history paralleled the decline and fall of New

York City's multiplicity of newspapers, from the great *Herald Tribune* to the *Telegram and Sun,* the *Journal American,* and down to the *Daily Mirror*. For a couple of pickled years he'd perched at the *New York Times,* and through it all he'd tracked the streets, the police stations, the halls of city government, in order to dig out the real facts. Now, in the twilight of his career, he made up facts.

We walked together to Nathan's door, paused, listened for sounds of whistling darts. Upon hearing none, I knocked and we cautiously entered, each of us trying to angle in back of the other.

Nathan was seated at his desk, a pile of newspapers in front of him, which I recognized as those of our competitor. "They're way ahead of us." Nathan slapped his hand on the pile. "Way ahead. You know why? Headlines. Their headlines are terrific. Listen to this —" He picked up one of the papers, read aloud from its front page. "We Love Our Two-Headed Sister. The person who wrote that's a genius." He tossed the paper aside, picked up another one. "Look at this one. Renowned Surgeon Accidentally Changes Man Into Woman. Now that's a story. Guy goes in for a hernia repair and comes out with a sex change. Why don't we have headlines like that? What's our headline for this week?"

Hip gazed bleary-eyed toward Nathan. "A UFO Ate Our Daughter."

"Not bad." Nathan pondered a moment, then looked up at us again. "But what if we switched it around? What about UFO Found In Girl's Uterus? Hip, take this down." Nathan stood, walked to his window and began to dictate. "Doctors are takin' a routine X-ray of a fourteen-year-old cheerleader with indigestion and they find a little spaceship. They operate and the thing flies out of the operatin' room. Down the hallway and out through the window. When questioned later, the girl can't remember it havin' flown into her, but admits she sleeps with her legs open."

Hip was scribbling in his notebook. When he finished, he looked up, and said, calmly, "Fine, we'll run it."

"It reaches out to a bigger audience," said Nathan. "Do you see what I'm drivin' at?"

"Anything you want, Nathan." Hip reached out a hand, steadying himself with the edge of Nathan's desk. Our publisher lifted his pudgy rump up onto the windowsill and peered out at a circling flock of pigeons. "My blowgun, Howard."

I handed him the instrument, said to Hip softly, "While he's loading, don't you think —?" I nodded toward the door, and Hip and I returned to our own wing of the office. Crumpacker was waiting for us.

"How do you like it so far?" he asked, handing his puppy story to Hip. "Am I on the right track?"

"Hip, this is Cardinal Crumpacker, our new editor."

"How'ja do," said Hip, crumpling down into his chair and opening his medicine bottle.

"I became very involved," said Crumpacker. "She starred with a German shepherd in a Tijuana nightclub, and before she knew it —"

Hip glanced at the first two lines and handed it back. "Good enough." It was not Hip's policy to be overly critical of the stories we concocted for him, so long as they had the correct number of lines. Crumpacker looked puzzled. "But you didn't even get to the part about the hormones."

I put my hand on his shoulder. "We will, old man. But the essential thing is the headline, which we already have."

"Well, why don't you just fill the paper with headlines?"

Hip O'Hopp chuckled mournfully and turned to his computer. Crumpacker looked at me. "What's he laughing about?"

"Headlines are the hard part, Crumpacker."

Crumpacker looked down at the lineup of headlines on Hip's computer screen, beginning with A UFO Ate Our Daughter, now being amended to UFO Found In Girl's Uterus. "Well, it seems to *me* you just have to think up *any* crazy thing."

"Yes, Crumpacker, indeed. Except all the crazy things have *already* been thought up by all the other newspapers just like ours."

Crumpacker pointed to a paragraph midway down the page. "Do you mean to tell me someone else has described the anguish of registering five German shepherds in the Tijuana public school system?"

"We must all be happy in our stories, Crumpacker, whatever that happiness is." I glanced at my watch. The morning was gone. I picked up Hip's phone, dialed Amber's desk and watched her answer. "Can we have lunch today?" I asked in a whisper.

"I have shopping to do."

"You never have lunch with me anymore."

"That's because you always do something to embarrass me."

"You are referring, no doubt, to that isolated incident when I administered the Heimlich maneuver to the old lady at the next table who was merely readjusting her dentures."

"I'm sorry, Howard, I know it's not your fault, it's just that you're an eccentric."

"Amber, I'm steady as a rock."

"You're the most notorious neurotic on the East Coast."

"I love the outfit you're wearing today."

"What color is my skirt?"

"So taken was I with the *way* you're wearing it —"

"Forget it," she said, sighing into her mouthpiece. *"I'm not having lunch with you."*

"Someone else, then?"

"That's my business."

"What if I follow you?"

The phone clicked in my ear as I watched her hang up with a little shake of her shoulder-length curls. Her jaw was like something created by the smooth hand of Erté, her neck long as Pavlova's, her beauty flawless, really, but she was not so young as Celia, and she worried about decline and decay, a consideration made stronger by the place of her employment, for Chameleon Publications, whose publisher was at this moment aiming a blowgun at a pigeon, left much to be desired for a beauty editor. As its editor in chief, I represented all the wrong things, I suppose. But eccentric?

■   ■   ■

Hip O'Hopp and I left the building at lunch hour together and walked up Sixth Avenue. On both sides of us flowers and leaves reached out, forming a canopy of green. Workmen were busy tamping the soil, weeding the pots, staking the slender young seedlings with bamboo. Next door to Rain Forest Plants was the New York lottery, and we both entered, as we did each day. A few minutes later, with hope in our hearts, we resumed our march up the avenue, past the Indo

Pak Kitchen, the Olympian Gourmet Deli, the Corea Brothers hot and cold plates — all regular eating places of ours.

We turned on Twenty-eighth, past windows full of jade turtles, ivory unicorns, and turquoise horses whose silver bridles sparkled with little gem stones. Fate had cut us off from the prestige and perks of the regular corporate world, but as a kind of compensation we, like these supernatural creatures, lived in an arcade of dreams, turning out fairy tales for the modern reader. The day was what you made it, its shape open to innumerable interpretations, read all about it in the *Midnight Examiner*.

At Broadway we shuffled into the Hong Kong Express and ordered from a menu we knew by heart, then found our way to a cramped booth in back, on which a few dried noodles were sprinkled, as well as some leftover bits of rice. We wiped the soy sauce from the seat and sat, Hip across from me, looking like a tall, dissolute rabbit, owing to large, overlapping front teeth that slightly lifted his upper lip. "Ever been to an ass pricker, Howard?"

"So far as I know, I haven't."

"Chinese." He poked a chopstick. "Puts needles into you?"

"Acupuncturist."

"Quite a lot of them around these days." He glanced back over his shoulder toward the kitchen, as if suspecting one might be back there. "Said to work wonders on the human body." He turned back to me. "I've been thinking of going to an ass pricker who practices in my neighborhood."

"Something wrong?"

"She's a plump little Chinese lady, I bump into her all the time at the A & P. She's shown romantic interest. I'm thinking of my old age. Might be nice to have an ass pricker around. What do you think?" He sighted me over his water glass, which he'd half filled with gin from his flask.

"I don't think it's a solid basis for marriage."

"Ass pricking?"

"No, old age."

"I've seen how old people wind up in this city, Howard. I've found them stiff as boards, huddled by their radiators. After I can no longer write headlines, after what's left of my brain dissolves, that's the time for a plump little ass pricker to look after me. I have a vision of myself on the Bowery, draped in rags, clutching a bottle of Thunderbird as I rave about the Good Old Days on the *Trib*."

"It'll never happen to you, Hip."

"But how can you guarantee it won't?"

"Well, for one thing, I'd let you move in with me."

"I can't dismiss this ass pricker that quickly. She's a valuable resource."

"*Numba Five . . .*" We went to get our orders. The counter girl handed them to us, along with packets of hot mustard and other seasonings. "How you today?" she asked, smiling at Hip.

"What do you think of her for the long run, Howard?" asked Hip as we returned to our table.

"She's only a teenager, Hip."

"They have great respect for age in the Orient. Can't do enough for their elders." He glanced back at the counter girl, encased in his obsession, which for today was his old age. He turned back to me. "I'm in good position in the romance department, what with the ass pricker on one hand and Ursula on the other. Have I told you about Ursula? She works for NBC, and has a really wonderful hospitalization plan."

"Major Medical is a powerful aphrodisiac."

When lunch was concluded, we walked over to Seward Park, where we took our regular bench in the shade of a sycamore tree. Hip stretched his legs out, hands in his pockets. "I finished up badly with Miriam. The schoolteacher I've been dating? She had a great surgical policy, but that long summer vacation was a problem. Wanted to go *to the country on weekends*." He looked at me. "The country is all right in magazines, Howard. Picture of a hill, some trees, fine. But to go there and be trapped in all that peace and quiet?"

"It takes its toll."

"I don't want to end up on the Bowery, Howard, but I have a greater fear of ending up in the country."

"Pecked to death by robins."

"When I'm old and my time comes I want to be able to fade into a crowd." He gestured toward Broadway. "I want to die in the rush hour, with people stepping over me."

Two bums came through the park, fighting each other with forks. They fenced, twirling and feinting until one of them fell down in the grass, and then the other one shuffled on, fork held up in victory, tines pointing skyward, points shining. Hip took out his notebook. "UFO Captain Stabs Pedestrian With Sword Of Light." He made his notation and folded his notebook carefully into his pocket. "Shall we head back?"

We walked west on Twenty-seventh. "I've fought a good fight." Hip, gesturing vaguely to the day, the city. "I've finished my course, I have kept the faith. Timothy, four, verse seven, an Irish drunk quotes from his buried past."

"Crumpacker would appreciate three hundred and fifty words from you on that very subject."

"Who's Crumpacker?"

"Woman gives birth to puppies in Tijuana?"

"Was her name Crumpacker?"

"Not the woman, our new editor. Name of Crumpacker."

"A fine writer."

"He'll be needing articles from all of us for *Prophecy*."

"What's *Prophecy*?"

"Nathan's new magazine."

"A fine publication."

We'd reached the doors of our office building once more. A candy and magazine concession held the center of the lobby and the owner of it nodded to us, above a rack displaying all our creations in a row — a friendly little gesture he made us each month.

We rode to our floor. The reception area was empty, Hyacinth gone to lunch and no one covering the switchboard. It was lit up, no doubt with creditors, angry lawyers, offended readers, and Lucky Cross advertisers. I walked to my desk, in time to eavesdrop on a conversation between Hattie and Celia, Celia talking rapid fire while Hattie took notes for her next issue of *My Confession*: "My girlfriend and her husband had this wonderful day together, and they were like really bonding, and then all of a sudden when she was making dinner he kind of got depressed and she said what's wrong and he said 'Why should I want to talk to you about it?' She looked at him like after twenty years of marriage, took this beautiful antique pitcher she had in her hands, and said 'Fuck you!' and threw it on the floor, *cracked* the pitcher, said 'I've had it with you, I've had it with this marriage, just go fuck yourself, what would I talk to you for, what do I look like standing here, just fuck you!' I couldn't believe it was Loretta talking this way, she said to me, 'I thought to myself who *does* he talk to, one of his like bimbos?' And I said how do you know he has bimbos Loretta, and she said 'because he fucks me differently.' "

Hattie leaned forward. "How does he fuck her differently?"

"He just does and she can tell, I couldn't even imagine how, but listen to *this* —" Celia's voice lowered, and I was forced to roll to the doorway of my cubicle.

"Loretta has this therapist, a very old man, very famous, and a few years ago he taught her how to get her husband interested in her again, he told her 'the other women aren't the issue, you are.' "

"What did he advise?"

"He said they should start *swinging!*" shrieked Celia. "The therapist said it would make him jealous, he said, 'look, men can only do it a few times a night, it's a physiological fact, but you can go all night long, and that will get him jealous,' it was like unbelievable, because Loretta was fifty years old at the time, but she's a really attractive woman, and she kind of dresses like a kid."

"Is she gray?"

"No, her husband likes brunettes so she dyes it. It sticks up kind of punk."

"Oh, well, she's cute."

"She doesn't wear a lot of makeup, she has real round cheeks, real pretty dimples, and is like kind of short, you know, but leggy, and wears wonderful clothes, interesting things, this really low belt with all these silver things on it."

"Good figure?"

"Yes, and tight black pants, and oversize silk shirts which sometimes she knots at the bottom."

They were off on a tangent now, one must be patient, the

entire wardrobe is being discussed, here they come back now:

"So, I said, 'did you *like* this swinging,' and she said it was kind of all right, it *did* get her husband jealous, but I didn't ask her the tales of swinging, if they were all four together or did they go in different rooms."

"Didn't you want to know?"

"Well, this was the first thing she'd really shared with me, and I didn't want to press my luck and make her feel she'd overshared."

Overshared?

"Anyway, that phase of swinging ended but she couldn't get past her anger with her husband."

"For being unfaithful."

"Yes, while she'd stayed at home for fifteen years."

"So that's the only way she was unfaithful, with the swinging?" Hattie, pulling for more.

"No, this is the really *interesting* part, her therapist said she would need to go out and find a lover because that would help her vent her anger, p.s. she *did* find a lover much younger than she, he's married, mid-late thirties, he was her TV repairman! I said 'what happened,' she said 'we got hot, we got interested in each other.' "

"Wonderful."

"But listen to this, she let the TV repairman buy her trinkets and presents, because the therapist said — I can't believe he said this *but* — he said 'you can always tell if someone loves you if they buy you presents.' " Celia tossed her long hair back, crossed her legs, leaned toward Hattie conspiratorially. "And the more expensive they are the better for you. When he buys you an expensive gift then you know he really cares, isn't that remarkable?"

"This is some therapist," said Hattie.

"He's eighty years old and very famous."

"I can see why."

"OK, so she had this affair with her TV repairman but p.s. she never had an orgasm."

"Never?"

"No, not with either of her husbands, not with any of the swingers, and not with her TV repairman. But — listen to this — she finally confided the Big One. She's been going out for the last year with some senior executive at Merrill Lynch who's seventy years old and *she's had the best sex of her life!*"

"Orgasms?"

"The only man who ever did it. They have lunch together a couple times a week, she's gone away with him a couple times, I don't know how she manages it."

"I don't know how *he* manages it, at seventy."

"He's in great shape, he used to be an athlete, she doesn't notice he's seventy, and p.s. she discovered oral sex with him. Well, I said 'if you think your husband fucks you differently when he's been with one of his bimbos don't you think he notices that after twenty years you've suddenly started to go down on him?' But she said no, he's like oblivious, he has no idea, none. She's positive."

"Does the Merrill Lynch guy buy her presents?" Hattie, using the latest theory.

"Yes, he adores her, he buys her things, she showed me a Hermès handbag, and he buys her very expensive shoes. And boots."

"And her husband thinks she's just a smart shopper."

"Right, he doesn't even know."

"He doesn't notice that she doesn't have orgasms and he doesn't notice what she's wearing." Hattie was facing her computer now, needing the greater speed of the keyboard to get the complete story down, 57 Isn't Too Late.

"Right," said Celia, "and there's more about this oral sex stuff with the seventy-year-old guy but we haven't really gotten into it."

"How do you know there's more?"

"She hints about it."

"Oh my god, this is fabulous."

"Isn't it something?" Celia's head was bobbing back and forth as she spoke. "She's so bright, such an amazing woman, she's just like opening up, something's happening to her, she has this rose aura around her."

Rose aura? I must get Crumpacker onto this for *Prophecy*.

"And, here's an interesting footnote, she wanted to fix me up with her TV repairman."

"But he's married."

"Yes, but he was going to leave his wife only now they have a new baby and he's not so sure anymore."

"It wouldn't hurt you to meet him." Hattie, always practical.

"She described him, but I didn't like him."

Well, we tried. Celia stood now, smoothed the front of her skirt down, and turned back toward her own desk, as I discreetly rolled toward mine, to write my Dr. Doris column, Oral Sex And The Seventy-Year-Old Man.

■　■　■

I was watching through my cubicle when Amber returned from a two-hour lunch. Posture statuesque, the aloof queen gliding. But weaving just a bit. There, bumped the edge of a desk. Drunk, not that I care.

She unslings her pocketbook, goes to her window, thoughtfully gazes out. Her phone rings.

"This is your editor in chief."

"What do you want?"

"Love may teach even a donkey to dance. Anonymous French proverb."

"You're not a donkey."

"What am I?"

"A good-natured zany."

"Well, that's something."

"Yes, but it's not enough."

"For whom?" (Thank you, Miss Wimple.)

"Howard, I have work to do."

"Have supper with me."

"No."

"Lunch tomorrow?"

"No."

"Coffee break at my desk, just the two of us, and the pickled twins?"

"Goodbye."

I watched her hang up. She sat at her desk, tilted her head back, long neck arched, and gave a little shake of her coiffure, to loosen any fragments of the conversation that clung to it. Head cleared, she leaned forward over her desk and went to work. Her copy was always on time, her articles straight and to the point, though at times Miss Agnes T. Wimple must correct her grammar, which Amber appreciates, don't we all? Indeed, she never feels bad about this, she feels deeply. "If you ever correct my grammar in public again, I'm going to strangle you."

I turned toward my own work. Here were my dancing girls, my pinheads. The afternoon lay ahead of us, we would circle, laugh, come pinheads, come to your editor, tell him to what new use he may put your unfortunate physiognomy. How about — Tribal Custom Insisted My Bride Be Veiled From Birth, Too Late I Learned Her Head Came To A Point?

I think I used that last month.

Taking out my little desk mirror, I looked at myself. There were large grease smudges on my glasses, odd I didn't notice them while looking out through the lenses. Getting slight pouches under the eyes, too much drinking. Nose aristocratic, don't we think? Suck in the cheeks, reveal the fine bones that hide. Overall appearance? Somewhat rumpled. However, *neglect is becoming*, Ovid, *Ars Amatoria*.

Dialing.

"Celia, dear, would you come to my cubicle for a moment?"

A beautiful young woman, Celia, and perhaps you're asking yourself why I'm not romantically involved with her, well here's why, I'm not comfortable with words like bonding. One has one's teeth bonded. One bonds two pieces of wood together with Bondo. This is bonding. When Celia speaks of people bonding I always see them joined together at the hip by birth defect, a pair of twins suitable for the pages of the *Midnight Examiner*. And that is why I'm not romantically involved with her, and it's probably why we've never bonded. However, I am about to *share* something with her, though I intend to guard against *over*sharing.

Here she comes, wearing a shirt like a floppy white accordion, and a pleated skirt of indigo blue, falling almost to her ankles. She's loosened her hair, it hangs almost to her waist, we'd been able to use it in a *Real Detective* photo, I Strangled Him With My Lovely Locks.

"Yes, Howard?"

"Sit down, Celia, please. May I say first that I love the outfit you have on today, especially that shirt."

"It's my seraphim shirt." She thrust her hands inside it, pushed out the yards of pleats. "I wear it like once or twice a year, I don't know why I had to have it. I thought I could always loan it to someone who's pregnant."

"Celia, Amber has just refused supper, lunch, and coffee break with me. Does she ever mention me at all?"

Celia ponders this. A serious girl, she will not answer without careful consideration. She lays a finger upon her cheek, she prods her memory, she turns back to me. "I don't think so."

"What does she talk about?"

"About getting another job." Celia crossed her legs beneath the long draped indigo folds and leaned back in the chair, elbows up on the edge of my bookshelf. "I just hung a young man. He's twisting slowly, slowly in the wind."

"A nice long, lingering death, good for a quarter of a column."

"He killed his girlfriend with a dumbbell because she forgot to put a quarter in his parking meter."

"Does that wrap the issue?"

"All done. Amber promised me the piece on her shit-burglar by five."

I swiveled toward my production board, and put a large X

through *Real Detective*. "You have a remarkable facility for this work, Celia."

"Sometimes I think it's pathological."

"It's a marvelous talent." I gazed into her dark eyes which, even when she wasn't speaking, continued to dance, looking left and right as if she had conspirators on either side of her, or was it her contact lenses troubling her? I had a blind spot about Celia, there was something in her character that kept eluding me. Her blood red nails clicked slowly on my bookshelf, in front of my collected volumes of medical freaks, carnival photo essays, and UFO sightings. "When interviewing for a job, Howard, do you think it would be better *not* to explain Chameleon Publications?"

"Opinions are divided on that question, Celia. I incline toward leaving off all mention of it."

It was time for the coffee cart. We walked into the hall together, and Celia stood before me on line, her soft scent mingling with the sugary aroma of butter strips and Danish. Hands in her pockets, spreading out the long folds of her skirt as she waited; and I, in my ill-fitting suit behind her, contemplating her form, airbrushing in her underwear, a harmless reflex.

Hattie came up behind me, whispered in my ear. "I Love The Coffee Cart Boy. How Can I Let Him Know?"

"A message in his buns?"

"Yes," said Hattie, "it might work." She smiled seductively at the youth, a young Latino with a shy manner. "A butter strip, please, Raoul, and black coffee, you must pose for us soon, don't you agree, Celia?"

Celia did agree, and sooner or later the young man's face would be used in dozens of ways by all of us — as an ax murderer for Celia, a feckless intern for Hattie's Young Nurses, a mystery teenage idol discovered by Yvonne, a young fisherman attacked by one of Hip O'Hopp's man-eating sharks (there was one in every issue), and finally I'd make him the bridegroom of a pygmy.

We walked back to our cubicles. I noted that Celia ate sensibly, a package of melba toast, and no more, while I stuffed sweet butter strips into myself like a gorilla, insulting my pancreas, catapulting my blood sugar, feeling much better, and now for some black coffee followed by two caffeine tablets, to carry me gently to quitting time.

■ ■ ■

Fernando, Hattie Flyer, and I stood at the bar of a nearby gin mill the staff frequented evenings after work. In a few hours it would become a topless bar, and on occasion I had been known to remain for this superb entertainment by an assortment of bored, tired, coked-out dancers, some of whom Melvin had photographed for *Knockers* and *Bottoms*. But now the stage was quiet, its silver streamers and colored pompoms hanging in shadow.

Joining us this evening for the first time was Crumpacker, long fingers wrapped gracefully around a martini glass; in the soft bar light he looked even more refined, while I by way of contrast was slouching on my stool, suit feeling wrinkled, shabby and hopelessly out of style, though I didn't know how. "Drink up, Crumpacker. Loosen your tie, relax a bit."

"I'm perfectly relaxed."

"Well, let me get you another martini, and see where that lands us."

Fernando opened his portfolio and removed some sample layouts he'd created to show to *Redbook* magazine, where he had a job interview scheduled. "How you like this one? Pretty snappy, heh?"

It was a drawing he'd made of a cow in a dress, apparently at work in a kitchen canning vegetables. It might have come from a South American women's magazine, circa 1942. "Perfectly rendered, Fernando. Very modern. Right in touch with today's woman. Wouldn't you agree, Hattie?"

Hattie hardly glanced at the layout, was intent on enjoying her after-hours cocktail. It had been a long day, and she had no interest, now or ever, in evaluating Fernando's cow in a dress.

Crumpacker removed a speck of lint from his sleeve and, with an impatient flutter of his fingers, cast it from him. "Today puppies, tomorrow guppies? I think I'm having postpartum depression."

"Happens to all of us, Crumpacker." I touched my glass to his.

Hattie was tearing off, like the petals of a daisy, the split ends of her hairdo. "I'm not getting enough fatty acid."

The bartender placed a bowl of greasy shrimp chips before her. "Try these."

She lifted one of the curling chips and looked at him through it. "I Became A Lush Because The Barman Was So Beautiful, But All He Gave Me Was A Bowl Of Chimp Trips."

"Shrimp chips."

"Whatever they are. Isn't he divine, Howard? We must get our cameras in here. Pose him beside that potted plant."

We nibbled our way through the shrimp chips, had another round of drinks, and then decided on more substantial food. "I shall cook," I said. "You will be my guests."

"They Called Me Barfly But What Did They Know Of Love?" Hattie unwrapped her ankles from the stool and climbed down unsteadily. Crumpacker and I each gave her an elbow and she tottered along between us, out to the street, light as a sparrow and tight as an owl.

The evening was balmy, the river nymphs channeling their perfumes through the smog, making the scent of twilight in New York. Crumpacker and I stood in the street, trying to hail a cab. "Adventure awaits us, old man."

"I must get home to my cats."

"Let the beasts prowl for an hour or two. Puts the edge on their appetite."

"They're Abyssinians. If they don't get their supper on time, they fling their litter around."

A cab hurtled toward us and screeched to a stop. Our driver was, as so many New York cabdrivers are these days, seriously deranged. He shouted viciously at other drivers, pedestrians, inanimate objects. Hattie attempted to engage him in conversation to slow his driving, and we learned that he lived in New Jersey, frequently slept all night in his cab, and had just purchased a hundred-thousand-dollar home in Tenafly, with a fireplace and swimming pool. "I've already been offered twenty-five thousand more than I paid for it." Window quickly down. "Eat your socks, you shitbag!" Back up, turning to Hattie. "I been saving my dough. I got it all figured out. I'm gonna be a real estate tycoon." Window down. "Get in the wind, motherfucker!" Window up. "Bunch of ragheads. They don't drive a civilized cab. They don't know *how*."

"Care for a mint?"

"Sure." Head out window. "You're an asshole one through

ten!" Head back in. "Why do I bother yelling? They can't speak English. Terrorists driving cab these days. Middle East greasers."

We were passing Forty-second Street. Hattie had her head against the glass, singing softly out of key, *"There's a broken heart for every light on Broadway."* I was looking at the movie marquees: EROTIC DREAMS SEX FEVER WET GIRLS HOT HOOKERS.

Hattie rolled down her window, gesturing loosely at the hordes surrounding us. "They're *life*. They're *vibrating*." She waved in the direction of a handsome Rastafarian drug peddler. I pulled her back into the seat and rolled up the window.

"Don't you read *Real Detective*? Most of the women found murdered in their apartments have let their attackers in voluntarily. No sign of forced entry."

"My god," said Crumpacker, "they've amplified those people." He was staring out his window at a revival stand erected on Eighth Avenue, where a potbellied crank in white linen suit and Panama hat was screaming into a microphone.

"THERE IS NO CITY TOO STRONG FOR US! NOT CAPHTOR, NOT HAZERIM, AND NOT, MY FRIENDS, NOT NEW YORK CITY WHERE GOD IS AT WORK TONIGHT! HALLELUJAH!"

"Crumpacker, interview that man tomorrow."

Our driver spied an opening and shot us through traffic, on up to Columbus Circle, which he whipped around with a fine disregard for the other vehicles circling with us. "Buncha commie chinks. You tell me, what happened to America?"

Broadway widened, traffic speeded up, we flew, up to Needle Park on Seventy-second Street. A young man stood there alone, smiling to himself, remembering a move he could make, something that would turn the wheel of his night one notch more, and he delighted in this realization, as his body made a faintly mechanical motion, jerked by the ultimate desperation that awaited him. We left him behind, spinning in his dream, and sometimes I think about strangers. "All these lives, Crumpacker —"

"I've got enough on my hands with two Abyssinians."

We had the lights timed now, speeding on, across the broad Eighty-sixth Street intersection; the old woman we almost ran down moved with amazing agility. We turned onto Eighty-seventh and stopped just east of the river, where Crumpacker had his digs. "I'll only be a moment," he said, climbing out.

The meter ticked on. Our driver gazed down the block. "Lotta spics in this neighborhood."

I wondered to myself, vaguely, about measuring his head, took out my notebook and pen. "Driver, I wonder — do you know your head size?"

"Adjustable."

Noted Doctor Finds It's True — The Criminal Skull Has Its Own Shape — *three simple measurements that could save you from marrying a murderer.*

"Spics and chinks."

Hattie leaned toward the front seat. "Anything romantic ever happen in this cab?"

"I've seen it all."

"Tell me the tenderest thing."

"One chick held a gun to my head and the other chick sucked me off. How's that for tender?" Looking up toward Crumpacker's door. "Where is this guy?"

"Feeding his cats."

"An old guy died in my building and his cats ate him."

Notebook back out.

". . . took the face right off him."

Kibble Runs Short, Cats Eat Owner.

"You have a pet, it should be in a cage. Hey, let's go, Mac!" Leaning on horn.

Here comes Crumpacker, without a trace of cat hair on his coat. He gets in, cab streaks forward, our necks snap backward, my cervical vertebrae realigning nicely, the ride has paid for itself.

We continued uptown on West End Avenue and at 103rd Street turned down to my place on Riverside Drive. Fernando paid the fare; I pressed another mint into the driver's palm as I stepped out. "Thank you for sharing your dream with us."

Hattie took her shoes off, as her ankles tended to turn over when she had a few drinks. She walked across the street and gazed at the river through the foliage of the park. The setting summer sun softened still more the faded rose print of her dress, and her hair took on a coppery glow. She was a woman alone, in spite of her escorts at sunset, and one could see it somehow, Hattie's solitary life. She'd loved too many lords of the manor house, too many cruel, dashing doctors, to ever be satisfied with the kind of single man she might find on the Upper West Side — a widower, perhaps, who ate yogurt at the corner restaurant. No, she must be ravished at the young nurses' station by a heartless intern who underestimates her, and whose life she saves later on by a simple nurse's trick, when he himself lies in shock upon the operating table.

I turned her from the poignant smell of the river and the distant sound of a teenage gang pounding on its drums. We walked back across the street toward my building — an old brownstone whose doorway was framed by two large concrete pillars. Beneath the small portico it was cooler. The ceiling overhead was curved and set with rosettes of dark polished wood. The door was glass protected by ornamental bars, with a wreath of wrought iron framing it. I fumbled for my key; we stepped into the old marble hall, and marched down a narrow corridor to the tiny antique elevator. I opened the creaking gate, we entered, and I pressed the button for my floor.

"I always feel like the Third Man in this elevator," said Hattie, and attempted to sing the theme in her thin, warbling, tone-deaf voice.

We rose slowly through the building and got off on the third floor. My apartment was just beside the elevator, and was ridiculously cheap for what I had — three very large rooms, railroad style, from a part of the mansion that had included gold leaf ceilings and large sunny windows with deep sills on which I'd placed my many plants. The floors were parquet, and the bathroom held a huge old tub and marble sink with old porcelain fixtures. The kitchen was modern, but had the quaint touch of an old casement window that cranked outward into a quiet air shaft. I had that warm, snuggly feeling of a satisfied New Yorker secure in his nest — a dangerous illusion, as we shall see.

We drank cognac on ice, and Hattie and I cooked lamb curry. We'd done it many times before, and never gotten the knack, for neither of us had a shred of culinary ability. Crumpacker kept a discreet silence throughout, but his gaze was critical. Finally, when it came to making the salad, he had to intervene and, grabbing the bowl, tossed the salad with impatient little maneuvers of the wooden fork and spoon. "How do you *exist* without fresh mint?"

"Only marginally, Crumpacker."

Fernando put on his favorite record, *Noel Coward in New York*. He loved Coward's fast patter, and each time he visited me he attempted to mimic it in a broken English gibber that resembled the conversation of a mother mongoose to her young. Dinner was served in a drunken haze. We sat at the kitchen table, overlooking the air shaft, from which a nice breeze came. Cardinal Crumpacker removed his jacket. "Crumpacker, at some point I'd like you to have a look at my wardrobe."

"Burn it."

Fernando kept turning to look at the wall. "I paint you a picture make this room come to life."

"See here, Crumpacker, there must be something to salvage from a man's entire wardrobe."

He extended his palm. "May I see your handkerchief?"

I handed it to him. He glanced at it momentarily, then threw it out the open window, into the air shaft. "The rest can follow."

"Well," said Hattie, touching my sleeve, "I think Howard's polyester suits are very attractive."

"To another polyester perhaps," said Crumpacker.

We had a Sara Lee banana cake for dessert, with whipped cream and peaches on top. It seemed to mellow Crumpacker. He said, "We might be able to save your socks. Let me see."

I lifted my cuff. Crumpacker sighted over his glass and shook his head. "Unacceptable."

Hattie lifted the hem of her rose print dress, rearranged it on her knee. "I wear what's comfortable." She narrowed her gaze at Crumpacker. "All my heroines do. In fiction one must be comfortable." Her elbow struck her wine glass, tipping it over. "Howard, open another bottle, I just spilled my drink in the bun basket."

Fernando staggered to his feet, crossed the room, and unzipped his portfolio. From it he took out a large charcoal pencil. He stroked its point with a jackknife, then charged the wall. I sat, as if in a fishbowl, and watched him begin to scrawl dark, violent lines on the huge white expanse. Crumpacker opened another bottle and poured for Hattie. "So how long have you been working at the office?"

"Ten years."

Crumpacker got a horrified look in his eyes, contemplating the decade ahead.

Hattie lifted her glass. "Nathan can teach you a lot."

"About what? Blowgun management?"

"May I point out that the two of you are just sitting there while Fernando is drawing on my wall?"

"Nathan gives a Christmas bonus." Hattie sipped her wine and gazed at Crumpacker over the rim of her glass.

"I can't imagine lasting that long. I mean, how many stories like the one I wrote today is the mind capable of producing?"

"Now he's dragging over the coffee table."

"Darling, the well is inexhaustible."

"Now he's standing on it. I suppose in order to reach higher, yes, that's it, there's going to be a fifteen-foot-high Cow In A Dress on my wall."

Hattie kicked off her shoes and lifted her feet up onto Fernando's empty chair. "I don't know where I'd be without the Whispered Promises Of A Dark Stranger." She wiggled her toes back and forth. "Even when I find out He's Been Married All Along."

"Well, at least there's Sara Lee," said Crumpacker, and shoveled the last pieces onto his and Hattie's plates. I was still staring in wonder at Fernando as he slashed along my wall, while singing his garbled imitation of Noel Coward. His pencil broke, he quickly razored it sharp again, and continued. I tried to rise from my chair, but some powerful force held me down.

"You get used to it," said Hattie to Crumpacker, "and then you realize you fill a special need for people. Let me tell you something —" She leaned toward Crumpacker. "I was traveling once, out in the Midwest. I stayed at a bed and breakfast. The son-in-law watched wrestling, had an eagle tattooed on his ass, and spent half of his time in the drunk tank. The daughter was about twenty-five and very attractive. She took twenty aspirins a day and had read every issue of *My Confession* for the last five years. I couldn't stand the thought of this nice young woman being so totally absorbed in my sordid fantasies, so I took her aside and told her to brace herself. Then I told her that I had written every one of those stories. 'Yeah,' she said, 'they do sound kind of alike.' And that was all. No shock. No anger. No feeling of being exploited. My stories were like her aspirin tablets. She took them to get herself through the day."

"Yes," said Crumpacker, "but are twenty aspirin tablets a day good for you?"

"If you've got a headache that won't quit, they are."

Fernando was pushing my desk over to the wall now, in order to stand on it and reach higher. I wanted to stop him, but whenever I eat Sara Lee cake I get loggish.

"So think of yourself as performing a healing service to your readers." Hattie laid an instructive hand upon Crumpacker's.

"I suppose one *could* derive a certain something from a story about one woman's triumph over the narrow-minded Tijuana school system."

The outline on my wall suddenly became clear. It was a woman reclining, her toes beside my bedroom door, her head near the archway to the kitchen. Her stomach was an enormously fat mound, inside of which Fernando himself could have fit. Her thighs were great huge slabs. Fernando turned, looked at me. "I need a model." He stepped over to Hattie. "Miss Flyer?"

Hattie looked up, peered around him toward the wall, rather the way she looked at his Cow In A Dress layout for *Redbook,* after which she returned her gaze to Crumpacker. "Your story contained a universal truth about public school systems everywhere."

"I make you the immortal Big Womans." Fernando knelt beside Hattie, charcoal in hand.

"If readers can find universal truth in *that* story they should be institutionalized." Crumpacker seemed unyielding on the point.

"Many of them *are* institutionalized," I interjected. "A good portion of our subscription list is from prisons and mental hospitals."

"I paint you like you never saw." Fernando took Hattie's

hand in his. "Please, Miss Flyer, before I lose my inspiration." He placed a kiss upon her fingertips. Hattie looked down at him.

"Fernando, what are you doing with my fingers?"

He began to kiss his way up to her wrist. "I make you a queen. You are Fernando's Big Womans. A Big Womans . . . cannot be made . . . without a beautiful womans . . . to model for her."

"I'm drunk, I'm tired, and I know where this kind of thing leads. I'll be running nude down Riverside Drive."

Fernando pulled an invisible garment from her with a violent wave of his hand. "I show the world the true womans."

"And I'll end up in the morning crouching in the park, trying to figure out where I've left my clothes. It won't be the first time, Fernando." Hattie gave a nervous laugh and finished the remaining wine in her glass. "May I have a touch more?" she asked, extending her empty glass to Crumpacker.

Fernando looked at Hattie. "I need breasts."

"We all need breasts."

"Call Mitzi Mouse." He thrust the telephone at me.

"Fernando, I'm sure Mitzi Mouse has other things to do than come here."

"She have the most beautiful tits in New York, and she come for Fernando when she hear about his great mural."

I dialed her, certain that she wouldn't come. We hadn't seen her since Nathan's brother, Melvin, had hired her for a special *Knockers* centerfold with himself as cameraman. His photographs of this gorgeous young woman were among the most grotesque any of us had ever seen, Melvin having spent the entire session photographing her breasts from only inches away, at such an angle as to give them the look of something out of a Brobdingnagian nightmare; the shooting would have been a complete loss had not Hip O'Hopp thought to run the photos in the *Midnight Examiner* under the title Angry Mother Smothers Puny Mugger With Bare Boobies.

Mitzi was at home. She remembered us, she was free for the evening, and seemed to like the idea that a painter needed her to model. *"I'll grab a cab."*

"When I was a teenager," said Hattie, "I was haunted by the Maidenform bra ads. There was one that said I Dreamt I Was an International Figure in My Maidenform Bra. It showed a woman in her B cup being greeted by a large crowd at the airport. I even remember the style of the bra. It was called Intermezzo." She glanced at Fernando, and I realized she was reconsidering, but she'd missed her chance, thank goodness; it would have been intolerable to wake up every morning to Hattie Flyer's tush six times larger than life on my living room wall.

We chatted, the sounds of summer night came on — muffled voices from apartments lower down the shaft, sirens from the street, music, barking dogs — and then — my door buzzer. I answered on the intercom, and Mitzi Mouse's voice crackled up to me. I buzzed her up and waited in the hall, as the ancient elevator creaked through the building.

She was a surprise to me as she stepped into the hall, for the girl we'd photographed for Chameleon Publications had been heavily made-up, with shades of gold and blue and green around her eyes; false eyelashes had given her the wide gaze of an Egyptian goddess; cheek blusher had lent strong contours to her face; her lips had been moistened with cherry red gloss. The effect of all this had been a dazzling mask. The girl who stood before me now had no makeup on, no false eyelashes, no moistened lips, no come-hither smile. Her long bleached blond hair hung limp; her eyes, though large, were framed by very light lashes and brows, which made them look both bald and surprised; her nose, which I remembered as having the aristocratic line of a Queen Nefertiti, was in fact slightly askew.

"I wasn't sure I had the right address, I lost it two seconds after you gave it to me." She walked past me, a little wan figure in a navy trench coat, the belt dangling loose in back.

"Here, let me take your coat."

I slipped behind her; she arched her shoulders and her coat came off in my hands. Her only item of clothing was a pair of high heels, in which she clacked down my hall. "I thought why bother getting dressed."

"Perfectly sensible." I gave her my arm at once, as one has been trained to do for a woman who's just arrived naked to a party, so that her entrance remains a simple statement of preference, rather than a thing too calculated or too keenly imaginative. We entered the living room, and Hattie Flyer's glasses slipped down her nose. "Such a lovely figure, don't you think, Howard."

"Mitzi, you know Hattie Flyer, and this is Cardinal Crumpacker, a prelate in the Holy Mail Order Church of California."

"Oh my goodness." Mitzi attempted, inadequately, to cover her copious breasts with her arms.

"Crumpacker's a radical new theologian, Mitzi. And here is Fernando, our artist."

"You are a goddess," said Fernando, taking both her hands in his. A naked woman tends to dominate a dinner party, the trembling aspic cannot compete with her. For a moment conversation faltered. I nervously searched my pocket for a handkerchief with which to clean my glasses, but Crumpacker had thrown it out the window. Mitzi turned to look at the wall, one hand on her hip, above the white line of an invisible bikini. "I can see just where you're going."

"A Big Womans." Fernando nodded, lit a cigar, and led Mitzi to the couch beside the wall. "I never forget you for this," he said, posing her on the couch. "Lean back against the cushion, like that. Ah, you are the Mona Lisa. Now, raise your knee, that's it. Hang your hand over it, *sí, sí,* you are a goddess, you know what I want." Mitzi's hair spread out against the cushion behind her head; those remarkable breasts that had, in Melvin's photograph, Smothered Puny Mugger, now arranged themselves in the most pleasing way.

Fernando studied her for a moment, cigar glowing between his teeth, then climbed back onto the desk and attacked the wall with his stub of charcoal. I poured a drink for our guest, and swung my chair in beside her. "What have you been doing with yourself, Mitzi?"

"Making a mess of things."

Fernando called down from the desk. "You going to be in the history books now, kid. Fernando's Big Womans."

"I'm already a Big Womans. There's a twenty-five-foot-high poster of me outside a movie marquee on Forty-second Street."

I sat forward in my chair. "Not *Erotic Dreams Sex Fever?*"

"You saw it?"

"We passed it just tonight."

"Well, I'm the star, if that's the word for it."

"I'll make a point of seeing it tomorrow night."

"Please don't." She paused, seemed reluctant to speak further. "Actually, I've been working on a poetry collection. That probably seems incongruous —"

"Perish the thought." I rushed to assure her that it wasn't incongruous, that indeed Elizabeth Barrett Browning, Christina Rossetti, Virginia Woolf herself, had all been known to remove their clothes at one point or another in their lives.

"The whole year's been one crazy scene after another," said Mitzi, "but I've managed to put this collection together somehow, and I think there are good things in it."

"Free verse?" asked Crumpacker, which surprised me, as I hadn't pegged him as a poetry buff, but there you are, they come in all sizes.

"Not exactly," answered Mitzi. "I wanted to prove I could do it, so I've worked in very strict forms, like the French rondeau, it's in octosyllabic measures." She gave her hair a brave little toss and straightened her shoulders, which thrust her glorious bosom forward in the most poetic way imaginable. I was terribly moved, as I always am when octosyllabic measures are mentioned.

She settled herself back into the cushions, and letting one arm fall languidly to the floor, asked, "What have you been doing?"

"We have a new magazine called *Prophecy*. Spiritual orientation. Cardinal Crumpacker here is the editor."

"Do you publish poetry?" asked Mitzi, turning her sweetest smile on Crumpacker.

"I don't see why not," said Crumpacker, looking at me.

"Crumpacker will take some, and I can squeeze a few into *Knockers*, you have no objection to being published in *Knockers*, do you?"

"Do you pay?"

"We usually pay by the knocker."

"That's why I do porn." She ran a hand along the outer edge of her smooth, tanned thigh, as if to remove some remaining veil and deposit it in the air.

"You're an intelligent young woman," said Hattie. "You could get a license to sell real estate."

"Hattie, why would she want to sell real estate?"

"She might find me a new apartment."

"I doubt it," said Mitzi. "I'm not much good at anything. I was a lousy waitress, I was hopeless as a receptionist, and I lasted only two nights as a barmaid. All I can do is take my clothes off." She ran a hand through her hair lazily, and I knew Hattie wasn't going to get anywhere as a guidance counselor. "Besides," said Mitzi, "I had to support my former husband, who was a starving painter." She sighed poetically. My gaze was drawn to the silken curls of her pudenda, which put me in mind of Tennyson's work.

"Tell me about your husband, Mitzi," said Hattie, trying to get a grip on her pen for some note taking. "How did he influence your life?"

"He took me to a camera club and I took my clothes off."

I looked at Hattie, who was scribbling drunkenly, and I knew the headline I'd be seeing tomorrow:

My Husband Made Me Strip For The Boys.

"Some of my friends said he was using me, but the truth is I like men looking at me, it's part of my basic insecurity."

"Why Do Those Cheap Glances Mean So Much To Me?" Hattie looked up from her notebook. "That's going to be our Reader's Confession Story of the Month, Howard. Give Mitzi a check for a hundred dollars."

"My husband suggested I'd be more photogenic with a

nose job, and he knew a doctor in Mexico who was supposed to be a genius, so we went down there, but he wasn't a genius." Mitzi sighed, turning her head sideways momentarily, with a finger to her nose.

"My Husband Said Get A New Nose Or I Get A Divorce." Hattie, finishing the issue.

"He loved the Mexican sun, and said it was his turn to be the breadwinner, he'd start selling Peruvian hammocks, they were real works of art, so he went to Durango and I never saw him again."

"Hammock Salesman Made King Of Jungle Tribe," said Crumpacker, as if suddenly waking from a dream. He looked around at us, quite pleased with himself.

"Crumpacker's risen rapidly, Mitzi. He possesses a great spiritual gift."

Mitzi drew out a strand of her hair, examined the tip of it. "I found a wonderful new shampoo. It's called For Virtually Destroyed Hair."

Hattie, whose hair seemed as virtually destroyed as any I've ever seen, ignored this timely consumer advice; her pen was making nervous little scratching sounds. "He dumped you in Mexico."

"I came back to New York, and tried to get into serious acting. There was this director, quite famous really, who asked me to dinner. He wanted to talk about my being in a new film of his. We were at the 21 Club, eating, when I suddenly remembered that I was due down in Chinatown for a modeling session with an old man named Mr. Wang. I called Mr. Wang to tell him I couldn't make it, and he made me feel so guilty about breaking our appointment that I left the director in the middle of the meal. My director never called me again and Mr. Wang didn't have any film in his camera. And after the session he offered me ten dollars more to give him a blow job."

Fernando's cigar glowed between his teeth, his charcoal moved rapidly, and the Big Womans's face, resembling some kind of blood-drinking Aztec deity, rose out of the archaic layers of his unconscious.

"How did you get into porn?" asked Hattie, digging for the essentials.

"I met another director and he said he had a part for me, only there was humping in it. But I said to myself what's humping, it's basic, it's poetic, it's the primal image."

"It's humping," said Hattie.

"Sure, but it's the friendliest thing two people can do. No crime, no violence, no greed. I know how silly it looks, but it's just tenderness really. When you look at it, all you see are people giving each other pleasure."

"It's humping."

"The Holy Mail Order Church issues its blessing," said Crumpacker.

I lifted my glass. "And that's enough for me."

"The only thing I don't like," said Mitzi, "is the producers. They're a bunch of gangsters. Tony Baloney's gang. They treat the cast like shit."

Hattie's pen continued to scrape. Fernando continued to draw. We all continued to drink, and the sounds of the city's night continued to murmur around us — the distant drums, the sirens, a ship's horn on the river, a man, somewhere beyond the air shaft, barking like a dog.

"**N**ow," said Nathan Feingold, "Cardinal Crumpacker here is in charge of *Prophecy*. He'll need full cooperation from all of you. Cardinal, I'm sure you'd like to say a few words."

"I can't think why," said Crumpacker, and that ended our conference. We returned to our various cubicles, and I invited Crumpacker into mine.

"What have you got lined up for the first issue?"

"A bunch of crazy nonsense."

"What do you think of the suit I'm wearing today?"

"It's you."

"Sit down, Crumpacker. As you are aware, there is a work in progress upon my living room wall. I wish I could feel more positive about it, and I was wondering if you, as a man of the cloth, had some words of guidance for me on it."

"Drapes."

Fernando appeared at the doorway of the cubicle. "What a Big Womans." He took a large cigar from his pocket, lit up. "Now —" He leaned over, both hands placed on my desk. "— I don't want you to pay for a thing. I cover all expenses."

"Good, because Crumpacker and I were just discussing some form of drapery."

"I pay for all the brushes, oils . . ."

"We were thinking a *large* drape, nothing fancy, but thick. Opaque, actually."

"All night I dream of my Big Womans."

"I had nightmares too. Now, we'll need a long rod and some brackets."

"I be there after supper." He laughed and slapped me on the shoulder. "I got to be with my Big Womans. She's lonely without her Fernando to sing to her." He marched off, puffing excitedly on his cigar.

"Well, what are you going to do?" asked Crumpacker.

"One mustn't appear crass, Crumpacker, one mustn't make a *mistake*. What if Fernando is painting the new *Demoiselles d'Avignon*?"

For the first time I saw hesitancy on Crumpacker's face. He wasn't certain, after all. He left me then, and Siggy Blomberg entered. Deep circles hung beneath his eyes; his face was pale. He plopped into my visitor's chair. "I didn't sleep a wink. I kept springing from my bed and charging around the room. I felt like I'd had fifty cups of coffee."

"Have a mint, Siggy. It'll soothe your nerves."

He popped one in his mouth. "I been hearing bells since

yesterday. My blood pressure feels like it's going through the roof." He stood, the last bit of color draining from his face as he did so, and hurried away, pants shining. I rotated slowly in my chair, past window, walls, and cubicle doorway.

"Howard, what are you doing?"

"I'm spinning, Amber, off into my future."

Our beauty editor stood in the doorway. I spun past her and the gallery of my grotesque photos, all the while contemplating an internal image of myself as an elderly cheesecake editor in a wrinkled suit and badly fitting toupee, spilling Geritol on his latest layout.

And back to Amber.

"Yes, dear, how may I help you?"

"What are you working on?"

"The Man Who Eats Cooked Sneakers."

"I'll trade you."

"What's yours?"

"Vibrator Runs Amok, Mutilated Woman Sues. I'm just not in the mood for that one."

"Very well, here's the Sneaker Eater — I'll just take your Vibrator."

"It's not *my* vibrator."

"No, certainly not."

I saw Amber looking down at my desk and followed her gaze. Siggy had forgotten his pen. It was a curious writing instrument, the liquid-filled barrel containing the photograph of a young woman in a bikini. Amber picked the pen up, studied it, tipped it over in her fingers. The fluid drained down, taking with it the girl's bikini. "How did I ever wind up in this place? The longer I spend here, the less qualified I am to work at *Vogue*." She was absentmindedly turning

Siggy's pen over and over in her hand, bikini rising and falling off the tiny maiden in the transparent barrel: Amber herself, dizzily spinning in the grip of fate.

"Lunch today?"

"No." She left with the Sneaker Eater story, and I turned my attention to the story of the woman whose vibrator had run amok. It was accompanied by a photograph of Hattie which Fernando had pulled from the files. We'd used it before, naturally, in the Woman Bitten By Mailman story, among others, but our readers have busy lives performing brain surgery, designing haute couture, translating ancient Greek, and they forget quickly.

From the corner of my eye, I saw the scurrying form of Siggy Blomberg returning to my cubicle.

"Did I leave my pen here?"

I nodded to it, and Siggy scooped it up. "Can't lose this."

"It's a beautiful writing instrument."

He looked over my shoulder at the computer screen. "Vibrator Runs Amok? What the hell is this?"

"A true story, Siggy, of one woman's terrible ordeal."

"You've got to be kidding me. You can't run this story."

"Why not?"

"Why not? You ask me why not? I'll tell you why not. Because these shit rags of ours are *filled with vibrator ads!*" He yanked a copy of the *Midnight Examiner* from my desk, whipped it open, and laid it before me. "A half page. Mr. Good Vibes, A Sleek New Tool For Tension Relief. They're a respectable vibrator firm, and they pay on time. If they see a story like this, they'll go through the roof." He looked back at my computer screen. "A lady gets creamed by her own vibrator, you must be nuts. Whose idea was this?"

"Hip's."

Siggy charged around the cubicle to Hip's desk, and began shouting. Hip looked at me, ran a finger across his throat, and I punched the DELETE button on my computer. Siggy positioned himself between our two cubicles. "I don't wanna make more work for you guys, I know you have to squeeze your kishkas to come up with this stuff, but I'm in the trenches every day with these fuckin' vibrators, I can't afford to lose a good client. You understand where I'm comin' from?"

I understood, and Hip was opening his tonic bottle and pouring himself a shot.

"I'll make it up to you," said Siggy. "I'll think of somethin' to replace it. How about — how about —" He scratched his head with his bikini pen. "Arab Woman Marries Camel."

Hip looked at me through the glass, his eyes focusing already on the possibilities. I nodded, and swiveled back to my computer. "OK, Siggy, you're off the hook."

Siggy hurried off, and I turned to the camel stables of Firuzkuh. I was deep in camel dung when Celia Lyndhurst entered my cubicle, sat down, and rearranged one of the ivory combs that held back her Rapunzel-like hair. "Howard, I think it's time I had a raise."

"Extra money is available to anyone on our staff."

"I don't like posing for those stupid confessions."

"You always look so charming in a nurse's uniform."

Celia adjusted the hem on her miniskirt, tugging it down, as if anticipating the angle from which Melvin would try to photograph her. "Have you heard from Kloss?" she asked; she'd been having an affair with him, up until Nathan sank a dart in his calf. Now Kloss was gone, and Celia hadn't been the same since his going. "I knew Kloss would hurt me, and I knew I'd have to play it out." She looked toward my window, her dancing eyes melancholy now, and a confessions mood coming over her. I heard Hattie's chair wheeling quietly toward the outer corner of my cubicle as Celia turned back to me. "Kloss and I met at an odd millisecond in time that may not provide for a clear transition."

Mystical stuff, Crumpacker's department.

"And I said to myself, right person, wrong lifetime. Do you know that feeling?"

As happens so often when listening to Celia, I hadn't the slightest idea what she was talking about.

"I recognized that he wasn't ready to commit, but I thought I'd take my chances. We used to spend our lunch hour in his apartment. The sunlight would come through the window onto his bed, and I felt like we were floating on the dust of angel's wings."

Hattie came around the corner on the creaking wheels of her posture chair and parked in my doorway. "You'll never get over that bastard until you drop the goddamned angel's wings."

"It was part of our courtship."

"Kloss was a prick and you know it."

"Hattie, we'd light *candles* and take *baths* together."

"He was still a prick," said Hattie, and wheeled angrily away.

"After lunch with Kloss, I'd come back inspired."

"I believe that was the period when all your murderers got reprieves."

"I couldn't pull the switch, not with springtime in my heart."

"Nowadays you fry them all."

"Sometimes I use lethal injections. You can always get two extra paragraphs of mounting tension with a lethal injection." She stood. Her gaze, though meeting mine, was seeing angel wings. I watched her cross the office floor, back to her own cubicle; Kloss's picture was pinned to her bulletin board, beside that of The Man Who Kept His Girlfriend's Head In His Refrigerator — actually a shot of Siggy Blomberg in a false mustache and goatee, taken by Melvin. We frequently used Siggy as a model, for he had a collection of toupees, received as partial payment from Mr. New Hair, one of our erstwhile advertisers.

It was lunchtime. I felt it necessary to treat Yvonne Plum, owing to our little contretemps of yesterday. "Yvonne, can I buy you lunch?"

I was standing at the door of her cubicle. She turned in her chair, fluffing out her wig. "Of course, darling. Just let me put a pin in Prince Rainier." She fastened a glossy photo of the aging monarch to her bulletin board. "I've gotten miles of copy out of the Grimaldis this month." She opened her compact, checked her lipstick and rouge, closed it again. "Monaco is four hundred and eighty-two acres of face-lifts, Howard." She picked up her handbag and took my arm, pressing her large breasts against me, just to let us know we were still alive.

We left the office and took the elevator down to the street. The sidewalks of Sixth Avenue were crowded with lunch-hour traffic. Yvonne kept her grip on my arm as we strode through the jungle of plants that lined the street. "I had such an uncomfortable morning," she said, "until I discovered I had my underpants on backward."

We entered a luncheonette owned by a tubby woman named Sonia, whose photo Yvonne had run in her magazine, identifying her as "the mystery figure" in the life of a young rock star who liked older, maternal women. Her husband toiled at the other end of the counter in his sleeveless undershirt, a cigar butt clamped in his teeth, his tattooed arms tossing a salad. "You need me for any posin' jobs this month?"

We'd used him in several *Midnight Examiner* features, most recently Crazed Husband Eats Wife's Gerbils, They Were Tasty He Says And I'd Do It Again.

"We might have something for you soon," I said. "We've started a new weekly."

"Yeah, what's it gonna be?"

"Religion."

"You're lookin' at religion." Lloyd lifted his arm and showed me the blue-and-red cross tattooed on his forearm. "And I got a cousin woiks sweepin' out a choich."

"We can use him too."

We carried our plates to the back of the little eatery and tucked in to Sonia's cooking. "Howard, do you ever think back to the days of Debbie and Eddie?"

"Never."

"Eddie was only twenty-seven when he was dating Debbie. And I was twenty-one. Why does lunchtime always make me wistful?"

"Because the day's half gone and so, my sweet, are we."

"I suppose that's it. But Debbie and Eddie —" Yvonne looked at me as she ate. "Things were steadier in those days. Those were the stars who were meant to be stars forever."

"And now so many are institutionalized."

"I wrote a story called This Is Mrs. Eddie Fisher Speaking. I was just out of college. Debbie and Eddie meant so much to me."

"The employment rate for old gossip columnists is much higher than for aging stars."

"I can't believe old Hollywood is gone. Where is Jeanne Crain? A gorgeous woman with red lips who was supposed to reign forever. I don't think I can go on eating."

"May I point out that at this very moment you are eating off my plate as well as your own?"

"I mean spiritually."

"Cardinal Crumpacker is our guide in spiritual matters."

Yvonne looked at me, seemed suddenly to grasp something moving deep in her mind. "Maybe I need a new wig."

"Shall we have dessert?"

"Make it something large and gooey."

I rose and walked back to Lloyd's counter. "Two large gooey somethings."

He handed me two plates, then stepped out alongside me at the edge of the counter. "You want me to shave my head so I'll look like one of them Hare Krishnas, I don't mind. It's show biz, right?"

I returned with dessert to Yvonne. Her eyes, as Hattie Flyer would have said in *My Confession*, were bright with unshed tears. "I'm never going to look at my old movie magazines again. It's a shock to the system, seeing June Allyson as a young girl."

"Eat your gooey dessert, Yvonne."

Melvin had his camera bag and tripod between his feet and was gazing quietly out the window of the cab at the city rushing by us; Celia was chattering to Yvonne. ". . . he said I should come to his party because this *man* was going to be there — a doctor, single, good-looking, that's all he told me, can you imagine trying to lure me to Tarrytown on such flimsy information?"

"You should go," said Melvin.

"Hopeless," said Celia, with a look toward Yvonne.

"Excuse me," I said, "I think it's worth a trip to Tarrytown. I mean, a doctor? Single? Good-looking?"

"They all think alike," said Yvonne.

Melvin and I gazed at each other, then at Celia. With an

air of great patience, she said, "A *woman* would have had *all* the info at her fingertips."

"What else do you need to know, for chrissakes," said Melvin. "He's a single, good-looking doctor. You marry him, he can take out your appendix for nothing."

"A woman would know if the guy's looking for a *committed relationship,* or is he just looking to fool around or cheat on the side. Who *cares* if he's a doctor, single, and good-looking if he's just looking to cheat."

The Chinese cabdriver spoke into his rearview mirror. "You take a shot at it, girly. Tarrytown not far."

We went down 103rd Street to the Drive and got out. Fernando had just stepped from his own cab, a ladder over his shoulder.

"Howard," said Celia, "I never knew you lived in such a nice neighborhood."

"Place going to be a national monument," said Fernando. We entered the building and rode up to my floor.

"Howard, I never knew —" said Celia of the hallway. "I mean, look at the flowers carved in the ceiling." A ceiling that soothes one after a difficult day. I opened my apartment door.

"Ah, there she is," said Fernando. "How you doin', baby? Did you miss me?" He patted the Big Womans on the hip. "I thought maybe I dream her. But here she is, in the flesh."

"She's certainly ugly," said Yvonne.

Celia glanced at the Big Womans, but was much more taken with the closet space I had. "Howard, such a *roomy* apartment." She had all the closets open and was standing on tiptoe looking onto the shelves. "Messy, aren't they?"

"They'll clean up. My entire wardrobe's being scrapped."

"You're not well organized, Howard." Celia straightened a few shirts, her delicate fingers smoothing the material in a way that Father Monkey never could. She turned toward me, her head doing a little Hindu dance. "I rearrange my closet every weekend. Take out all the sweaters and kind of line them up and do thicknesses on them, and colors, from wool to cotton to T-shirts, and they're piled up, and then you can run down them and see what you have, I can see my closet without opening it, I know just where everything is."

"I'll prepare a press release on this at once."

"It's called controlling your environment. When I was in college I couldn't study unless I cleaned my apartment for three hours, and then I could sit down and think for eight hours straight." She looked at me, eyes blinking with a contact lens flutter. "At this moment, do you know where your cotton balls are? Mine are in the fourth bureau drawer in the back, if you want an emery board it's the second drawer on the left behind the nail polish remover. But what I'm amazed by is how much *space* you have, it makes me realize how *inadequate* my place is."

"Yes, well, that's possibly why you have to be so organized, Celia, because your place is small, while I am able to spread out, you see, to luxuriate as it were, in my spacious, rent-stabilized apartment." With that little salvo, I left her and returned to my other guests in the living room.

Melvin was pacing back and forth in front of the Big Womans, camera bag still over his shoulder. Hattie had requested photos of the mural for her confession, I Supported Him While He Painted And Now That He's Famous I'm Forgotten.

Yvonne joined me at the liquor cabinet, but kept glancing

nervously over her shoulder at the Big Womans. "Of course I'm not an artist. I do know something about nervous break-downs."

Fernando spread his paints and brushes out on my desk. "When I put some color in her, then you see somethin'."

"Her tits are bigger than my head," said Melvin. He open-ed his camera bag and removed his equipment. Yvonne came and stood beside me as I gazed down into the kitchen air shaft, stiff drink in hand.

"You wanted my opinion so I'm giving it. Cover it with some nice fabric paper."

"Look at him, Yvonne. I've never seen Fernando so happy."

"He's had this horrendous thing inside and now he's get-ting rid of it. But it's going onto *your* wall."

"Perhaps it will teach me something."

"The only artist I ever had anything to do with made me roll around naked on a wet canvas. I got purple paint in my pubic hair and couldn't get it out for weeks."

A faint breeze was circulating in the air shaft, sounds of the building rising upon it, including those of my super, who lived in the cellar and spoke the word "Arrrgggghhh" with various shades of meaning at all hours of the day and night. He was speaking now.

"Is someone being murdered down there?" asked Yvonne.

"It's only my super."

"Arrrrgggghhhhhh . . ."

"With *that* in the basement and *this* on the wall —" Yvonne sat down at the kitchen table and combed her mod-acrylic bangs. Melvin was setting up his tripod, the falling legs making a soft sliding sound. "Even if I use the wide angle, I won't get it all in. Maybe I should use the fish-eye."

"Is my Big Womans." Fernando climbed up his ladder, lifted his moistened, oil-filled brush.

Celia came into the kitchen. "I'm going to go now before I die of jealousy." As I was showing Celia out, I met Mitzi on the stairs, her arms filled with containers of Chinese food. She was fully clothed in floppy sweater and wrinkled slouch pants, her hair up, silver chain earrings dangling from her ears, but again she'd left her war paint off and had the same bald, surprised look around her eyes. I took her containers, and set out plates. She helped me, slapping about the kitchen in a pair of loose sandals from which the laces dangled; I noticed that she was not well coordinated. "Yes," she said, after dropping lo mein on herself and opening a warm bottle of soda, which erupted on my ceiling. "I'm a klutz. I've always been that way." She blew a strand of virtually destroyed hair out of her eyes, and I wondered how she could even walk in those sandals, but she obviously functioned, moving along on a slovenly sort of willpower. Her focus was somewhere in her mind, on something she was desperately trying to see, which caused her to fall over her own feet, bump into me, lose an earring in the wonton soup. "And what magazine do you work on?" she was asking Yvonne, as she exploded a container of duck sauce on her sleeve.

"Movie gossip, darling. Got any?"

"Our producer is a Mafia creep. I'd sooner work for a harmless old degenerate like Mr. Wang than these gangsters." Mitzi dished out moo goo gai pan with a pair of soup spoons. "Tony Baloney drops people into the river in cement overcoats."

"You work for Tony Baloney?" asked Yvonne. "His family

used to run Brownsville. They wiped out the entire Mastachenza clan in Talerico's Clam House."

Mitzi fished an earring out of the wonton soup. "I'm humping this guy on camera for two hours straight, I'm worn out,
I'm sore, and suddenly there's a gun against my head. And
Tony Baloney says, 'You're not trying hard enough. Gimme
some passion.' " Mitzi clamped her earring back on. "I know
there's a poem in this."

"Kick him in the balls," said Fernando.

"I've got to transmute him."

"A kick in the balls transmute him," said Fernando.

I opened my fortune cookie. *Don't hesitate to correct er-
rors.* I looked up to my living room wall. Horrendously grotesque as the painting itself was, I had begun to enjoy the
excitement of a continuing party and felt I could not act on
my fortune cookie instructions, which was a mistake, always
obey your fortune cookie, it is as disinterested an adviser as
you're likely to have.

"Mitzi," called Fernando, "you ready to do some more
posin'?"

"Sure," she said, and walked over to the couch, where she
removed her baggy pants and sweater. I heard Melvin's eye-
balls make a sprocketing sound, and even Yvonne's eyes
opened wider at the sight of Mitzi's body. "Oh god," said
Yvonne quietly, "why do her breasts have to stand up so
straight?"

"It has something to do with the year she was born, dear."

"And I go all the way back to the Roosevelt administra-
tion."

I took her hand in mine. "Yvonne, you're an eternally
beautiful gossip columnist."

She laid down her chopsticks, then smiled suddenly, as if remembering some secret strength. "Liposuction. Tit-lift and tummy tuck." She raised her wine glass. "Oh Howard, at times of crisis it's so important to remember the really important things in life."

Melvin was bent over Mitzi, his camera inches from her breasts. "I've got an Ansel Adams shot here . . ."

Yvonne and I cleared the table, and she suggested a walk on the Drive. It was twilight, and the lamps of the park had just come on; beyond them was the Hudson, moving silently along. Across it on the Jersey shore the windows of the high-rise apartments were bathed in the glow of the setting sun. Were I a baboon this would be my hour of worship.

". . . being married to an East Side dentist has given me some of the best bridgework in town," Yvonne was saying, as we walked down the winding Drive, "not to mention a great feeling of security, but sometimes, Howard, sometimes I wish I'd married a bookie I once knew." Her hand rested lightly in the crook of my arm. Strands of her wig touched my cheek, and we continued on in silence then, letting the twilight influence our thoughts and feelings, Yvonne's of her bookie, and me of my Big Womans.

We descended the narrow corridor of the Drive, to the Fireman's Monument, where a young Latino crackhead sat, a curling plume of fried ideas rising from his brain. We walked on, past the curving Peter Stuyvesant building, and the building called the Cliff Dwelling, circa 1916. If you turn and look back in the twilit hour, you can see the old ghosts of Manhattan pulling up in their horse drawn carriages.

"I smiled too much today," said Yvonne, rubbing her face. "I feel like my jaw is coming unhinged."

The Drive was sloping up now, to the Soldiers and Sailors monument, where a display of stacked cannonballs decorated the lawn, lamplight glinting off them. Yvonne and I walked across the flat stone patio of the monument, in which a sealed iron door was set, the door to nothingness. An elderly black man materialized from its shadow. "I was in the First Worlds War," he said, staring straight at me. "Where was you?"

"I hadn't been born."

"You was in France with the Magnetic Line, but you didn't turn the guns aroun' and Mistah Hitler come up *behind* the guns. I don't give a fuck about ya no mo'. George Washington be fightin' here yet wittout me."

He looked in my eyes, the pupils of his own eyes burning with the fever of all the wars that had blended in his soul. He was dapper, well groomed, glaring out from beneath the brim of a faded fedora. "The battleground gonna be the United States and I don' give a fuck no mo'." He reached in his pocket, took out his wallet, and opened it to his veteran's card, wrinkled as he was and bearing the names of foreign lands. "America say go ahead Hungarian, start a revolution, I'll be there to help you, and they ain't showed up yet. *You* gonna get a revolution started on yo' ass, you be shittin' blue turds." He slapped his wallet closed. "Our boys crawlin' across no-man's-land into machine gun nests and I'm listenin' to this bullshit? America finished."

His eyes held me; one does not look away from the aged oracle when it speaks from the doorway of its temple. "I'm goin' down, brother, I got one life and I'm goin' down. I'm the backbone of this country." He came to attention. "Time is up on yo' ass." He turned and walked on, down Riverside Drive.

We started back through the twilit haze, with the air turning slightly cooler now, and the smell of the river reaching out to us. "In L.A., Howard, the breast-lift clinics have valet parking." Yvonne, pensive at sunset.

We returned to my building, and reentered the quiet lobby. It was a self-satisfied hall, accustomed from its earliest beginnings to gentlemen and ladies of good breeding coming and going through it. Now, its disapproving gaze chilled my neck, and I hustled Yvonne into the elevator. The spirit of the house was sternly watching me. *What's that Big Womans doing on my wall?*

When we entered the apartment, Melvin was still bent over Mitzi, camera clicking. She'd fallen asleep, with one leg drooping off the couch toward the floor.

Fernando was standing in front of the Big Womans. His two arms were raised from the waist, elbows bent, index fingers pointing toward the wall, as if measuring something. His body was perfectly still. His eyes were glazed. I passed my hand in front of them, and they did not blink. I pressed down gently on one of his extended wrists. His arm went down, but when released it sprang back up into place, still pointing at the wall.

"What's goin' on?" Melvin was beside me now. "He in some kind of trance?"

"Howard," said Yvonne, "his breath is very shallow."

Mitzi Mouse had wakened. "What's wrong?" She came toward us, tripped over her sandal laces and stumbled against me; I caught her naked body in a moment of Erotic Dreams Sex Fever, but had to release her in favor of Fernando, whose face was turning blue. Melvin and I took hold of him and lowered him to the floor. His eyes remained open, his arms extended, fingers now pointing at the ceiling. What had he been measuring? What part of the Big Womans's anatomy had triggered this seizure?

I slapped him lightly on the cheeks. "Fernando . . ."

"Here," said Melvin, "lemme try this." With my soda water dispenser, he squirted a bright bubbling stream onto Fernando's brow. "Hey, Fernando . . ." Melvin shook the reclining painter by the shoulders, then pressed down on one of his extended arms, but the moment he let go it sprang back into position, pointing at the ceiling.

I looked at Yvonne. The same headline seemed to be running through both our minds. Painter Sticks Two Fingers In Air, Dies.

"Let me try," said Mitzi. She knelt beside him, put her hand behind his head. "*Fernando,*" she cooed softly, "Fernando, honey, it's Mitzi." She lifted his head up, pressed him to her breasts. His extended arms pointed out on either side of Mitzi's body, and his nose disappeared into her cleavage. "Time to go to work, Fernando," she said softly. She looked up at us. "Genius is so unstable." She rocked his head back and forth, rolling his face in her soft flesh. Such intimate attentions would have wakened a *Knockers* reader from the deepest of drunken slumbers, a club on the head, or full anesthesia after appendectomy with the stitches still new, but Fernando remained rigidly unconscious.

Yvonne felt for a pulse on the outstretched arm. "I can't find anything."

I rolled him over, and began artificial respiration. His body felt like a lifeless sack. The Big Womans gazed down at me as I attempted to revive her prostrate creator. What monstrous power did the creature possess?

"I . . . can't seem . . . to get . . . him going . . ." I was breathing heavily and beginning to feel a sense of panic, but one of us, thank goodness, had presence of mind: I could hear Melvin's camera clicking, recording it all for the office files, for use at a later time.

"Let me in there," said Yvonne. "I'm married to a dentist." She shoved me out of the way, rolled Fernando on his back, and began mouth-to-mouth resuscitation. Her wig covered my view of their lips, but I could hear the steady current of gossip-laden life force flowing into Fernando. His leg twitched, his stomach heaved, and finally a groan came out of him. Yvonne lifted her head, and he blinked his eyes.

"How you doin', kid."

"Howard, give him some brandy."

I selected a moderately priced eau-de-vie and put it to his lips. He sipped it, then sat slowly up. "Where is my Big Womans?" He looked around my shoulder toward the wall. "Ah, there she is. Guess I fall asleep, huh?"

"You was stiff," said Melvin. "With two fingers stuck in the air."

Fernando got slowly to his feet, and dug into his pocket for a cigar.

"Fernando, old man —" I struck a match and put it to his cigar. "I don't wish to alarm you, but you had two fingers in the air and were stiff as a rake. Yvonne couldn't find your vital signs."

"You look for the wrong one," said Fernando, and winked at Yvonne. Then he turned to me and shrugged. "It happen to me sometime."

"What happens to you?"

"I black out." He snapped his fingers. "Just like that."

"And then what?"

"I wake up later."

"How much later?"

"Sometime I be walking along on the West Side, and I wake up later on the East Side. And I don't remember nothing in between."

I sat down, exhausted. My eye turned toward the Big Womans. Her hideous face was gazing back at me, her enormous black eyes dancing.

Fernando had picked up his sketchbook, and was looking at Mitzi. "We go back to posin', huh?"

"We're going to help you finish your great mural," said Mitzi, settling herself back onto the couch. "Nothing will get in our way."

I was, of course, gratified to hear this. I'd always wanted an epileptic painter in my life, arms extended, fingers measuring the infinite corridors of brain seizure.

"You my inspiration, baby." He was sketching Mitzi now. "I never seen nobody's got what you got."

The man had been catatonic only moments before, and now he was puffing away at a cigar. Had I been rigid with two fingers in the air, I should desperately want to know why. I'd be in a taxi headed for the emergency room. But there you have the difference between a mad Spanish artist and a sane American editor. Sane? I see your point.

"Matter of factor," said Fernando, "you take me tomorrow to this producer guy who's botherin' you and I tell him where to get off."

"Maybe you should go to see this doctor friend of mine." Mitzi was smoothing out the tasseled edge of a cushion, as if it were a troubled brow. "He deals with a lot of creative people. You should let me take you to him. Howard, you'd come along, wouldn't you?"

"I chit on doctors." Fernando, responding.

"I think he could help you, Fernando. You shouldn't be blacking out like that, it's not normal."

"I chit on normal."

"I'm going to call him tomorrow and we're going to see him."

Melvin was changing film in his camera, in preparation for another round of distorted close-ups. Yvonne was gathering up her purse and preparing to leave. "That wall of yours is just the beginning."

"What do you mean?"

"Good night, darling. Don't drink too much." She pecked my cheek and slipped away. I made an enormous drink for myself and walked back to the living room.

"I admire Yvonne," said Mitzi, as I sat down in a chair near her. "She's a very strong person."

I handed Mitzi a drink, which she sipped, some of it spilling on her chin, and a little rivulet dropping down between her breasts. "I'm not strong at all," she said, wiping her chin with the back of her hand. "So I rely on rash acts."

"I got a shot here is a masterpiece," said Melvin, his camera aimed up between Mitzi's feet.

He was a Park Avenue psychiatrist, and his waiting room was spacious and comfortable. We parked ourselves on a deep sofa, between two antique tables bearing Japanese vases with careful flower arrangements in them, bespeaking sanity and calm. The large expanse of wall across from us was pale peach, and Fernando was staring at it.

I noted the magazines on the coffee table before us. *Town & Country, House & Garden, European Travel & Life, Connoisseur*. Where was *Macho Man*?

"He's going to ask you all about yourself," said Mitzi. "And you tell him everything."

"I chit on everything."

"Be sure to tell him about your blackouts."

"I chit on blackouts."

I put my hand on his shoulder. "Fernando, Mitzi has gone to a lot of trouble for you. Tell Dr. Schotzky whatever he wants to know, and don't chit on anything."

"Chit."

Schotzky's receptionist came out from her area then, and summoned Fernando. He gave us a wink, and followed her into the inner sanctum.

"Well," said Mitzi, "we got him here."

"How did you swing an appointment so quickly?"

"I traded my appointment for Fernando's."

"You see Dr. Schotzky regularly?"

"He's helped me a great deal." She gave me a silky smile that could only have appeared with the makeup she wore. The goddess had returned, in a short leather skirt, a beaded Mexican shirt, a red beret. I noticed that her movements were more graceful now, she hadn't tripped over herself once, hadn't broken or dropped anything. Did her makeup and clothes create an image that her body followed obediently, mesmerized by its own beauty?

She was speaking of her poetry. I'd prepared myself with a few bits of Yeast, I mean Yeats. I cleared my throat, and after a pregnant pause, I let fly. *"How many loved your moments of glad grace, and loved your beauty with love false or true, but one man loved the pilgrim soul in you . . ."*

Mitzi opened her purse. "Look what Fernando gave me. Pretty, isn't it? The scrollwork?"

A handsome weapon, as automatic pistols go. The inscription on the barrel, *Fabrique Nationale D'armes de Guerre Hersial Belgique,* was decorated with raised leaves and berries. "Very nice," I said, handing it back to her.

"Can you feel its glad grace?" She held it up to the light of the table lamp. "So civilized on the surface, so polite, and so deadly."

"Loaded?"

"Naturally," she said, returning it to her purse. "Otherwise it's just a souvenir." She leaned back in her chair, and stretched her arms out wide. Her little sequined shirt rode up over her belly, and her navel peeked out. I opened my notebook and quickly scribbled, *Belly Dancing Saved My Marriage*.

"What are you writing?"

"A sonnet."

We chatted about the fourteen-line form until Fernando came out. "I'm gonna be a spearmint."

"A spearmint?"

"He find my case fascinatin'." Fernando took out a cigar, lit it, and led us out into the hall. He had a new air about him, of one who'd suddenly become valuable to science. We descended in the elevator and stepped out onto Park Avenue.

"Well?"

"He say I'm quite the guy. Say —" Fernando blew a thin stream of smoke into the summer air. "— say he never seen nobody like me before."

Mitzi put her arm through his, asked him gently, "Did you tell him all about yourself?"

"Whole story of my life. He really like the part about the chickens in the bathroom. I ever tell you about them? Started when I was ten year old. Every time I go into the bathroom I see chickens. Cluck around, then go out past me and then disappear."

"You still see these chickens?"

"We get along fine. Only thing is they don't lay no eggs."

"What did he say about your blackouts?"

"He say I'm schizofrantic."

Fernando strode along between us, a certified schizofrantic who saw chickens in the bathroom. He was smiling, head back, breathing deeply of the summer air, totally confident, filled with good will, ready to roll wherever the wheels of fate sent him, his hallucinatory fowls following after him. "That doctor know a lot about art. Showed me a bunch of pictures he got, nice little ones in black ink. Ask me what I thought of them, say it's very important. I tell him right off they're great, he got a valuable collection there. Every damn one of them is of a cow in a dress."

■ ■ ■

We dropped Mitzi off at the midtown studio where she was shooting her film for Mr. Tony Baloney, and continued on our way to Chameleon Publications, where I went straight over to Hattie and performed a charade for her, arms extended, pelvis snapping.

She studied me. "My Husband Wears My Clothes?"

I shook my head, turned, revolved my rear end around. Hattie rested an elbow on her computer, studied me thoughtfully. "Mother, I Love A Male Stripper?"

I put my hands on my hips, rotated them still more vigorously, up, down, and around, until my knees started to quiver.

"Belly dancing?"

I nodded, urged her on as I pirouetted, hips still rotating.

"Belly dancing . . ."

I took out my bankbook, waved it at her.

". . . savings . . . saved!"

I extended my arm, hummed the wedding march.

"Belly Dancing Saved My Marriage!" She turned to her computer and I staggered to my cubicle, thighs aching, in time to meet Crumpacker there.

"I've got the first five *Prophecy* articles." He indicated the manila folder in his hand. "I don't suppose you want to see them."

"Quite right."

"I worked *very* hard on Satan Made Me Saw My Sister In Half."

"Perfect for the *Midnight Examiner*."

"Well, it's going into *Prophecy* because I'm *not* giving it up."

"There's no need to give it up. Just make a copy of it for Hip and he'll rewrite it for the *Examiner*. You must think in terms of the group, Crumpacker. It's the only way we can churn out these magazines and still have time left over for shopping in the afternoons."

A faint look of incredulity still played upon Crumpacker's face. "We duplicate each other's stories?"

"Whenever possible."

"Don't the readers *notice*?"

"When they read a bogus story in two places, it becomes a fact. It's the secret of journalism. Really, Crumpacker, I would have expected a prelate of the Holy Mail Order Church of California to have a quicker understanding of the nature of our operation. And now you must excuse me." My intercom was buzzing, a summons from Nathan. I left my cubicle and went to his door, opened it with my body pressed flat against it, so as to leave less of myself exposed, a small advantage but one that could prove crucial, see *Kloss Pennington vs. Chameleon Publications.*

"Howard, we're being sued for twenty million." He indicated a legal document on his desk. "I'm wondering if there's a way to avoid these things."

I picked up the brief, and saw that the wounded party was a middle-aged movie queen whom Yvonne had slandered in the most salacious way. Nathan flicked his intercom on. "Yvonne, come in here would you, please?"

"I'm busy."

"I'm being sued."

"What else is new?"

"Just come in here, Yvonne." Nathan clicked off and turned back to me. "Someday she's going to bring this great publishing empire down on our heads."

There was a cautious knock, and then Yvonne entered, sideways. Seeing Nathan unarmed behind his desk, she turned full on and came toward us, her proud bustline uplifted and uplifting, molded in the lacy black knit of her sweater.

Nathan sprinkled bromide powder in a glass of water. "You have Lorna Lee in the locker room of a professional basketball team."

"She likes tall men."

"Then you have her in a motel with a TV preacher."

"She found Jesus."

"She found a lawyer who's squeezing my balls. You've got to keep your stories like cotton candy, remember? As soon as you get your lips on it, it melts. Ain't that what I've always told you?" He finished his bromide and set it down. "I'm surprised I have to tell this to an old pro like you,

Yvonne." Nathan put his hand to his mouth, belched. "Look, we've all been here a long time. We know what we're doin'. This Donald Duck lawyer can go crap in his hat. But let's not make life easier for him anymore, OK?"

Yvonne squared off to counterattack Nathan, and I returned to my cubicle, where I found Siggy Blomberg with eyebrows singed, waving a plastic Jesus night-light, its prongs black with soot. "I plugged it into the wall and the frigging thing exploded in my face."

"I told you never to test our products."

He nodded, rubbing his singed eyebrows. "Anyway, I've got *Prophecy* covered. Sold out every inch of space for the next six weeks. Religious trash and hernia supports. But Nathan wants to know why I can't get full-page ads for Bijan perfume." Sig tossed his scorched night-light on a stack of *Midnight Examiner*s. "These mags are for yekls, not ladies in sables." He opened his collar, ran a finger around his sweating neck as he gazed toward the sun-baked street. "It's like Dubinsky's Steam Baths out there and I gotta go hustle."

"What about that modern invention, the telephone?"

"You think Lady Rana of the Lucky Coin Medallion answers her phone? It's like trying to get a message from the dead." Sig fanned himself with a file folder. "I got to go there, up two flights of stairs where you're liable to get killed any hour, day or night, and threaten her. Here —" Siggy reached in his pocket, handed me a coin suspended on a chain. "Guaranteed to turn your neck green."

I looped the chain around my neck and settled Lady Rana's Lucky Coin inside my shirt. Siggy leaned forward, resting his elbow on the edge of my desk. "You open up a door in midtown Manhattan you're liable to find anything behind it.

I open those doors, Howard, I step through. I find myself in a skin blotch factory, one big room with a vat in the middle of it, bubblin'. Bubblin', Howard, with Blotch Cream, and some old guy standin' over it, stirrin' it with a baseball bat. I make up his ad for him, I write it, paste it, I'll do anything to sell space. Blotch Cream, Howard, I'm one of its creators, I dropped a wad of chewing gum in the vat and the old guy said it didn't matter, lots of things fall in."

"Does it remove blotches?"

"I got the end of my tie in the vat." Siggy lifted his tie up to me. "See that? Bottom's completely white. Next time I go back I'll throw the whole thing in, even out the color." Sig gazed thoughtfully at the end of his tie. "If a rat drowned in the Blotch Cream, he'd just get boiled down and put in a jar."

"Sig, maybe someday I should go on your rounds with you."

"We'll visit Madame Veronique of Voodoo Afrique. Ever see her ad?" Siggy opened a *Midnight Examiner* and showed me a half-page spread offering love potions, doll magic, protection stones. "She's into us for five grand already, but I let her slide because I don't wanna wind up beside a dead frog in a bottle."

I had, quite suddenly, a vivid picture in my mind, of a shrunken Siggy Blomberg floating inside a bottle, his curly hair adrift, his eyes wide and staring, as his hands reached out to the glass. "Come now, Sig, you're not really afraid of her, are you?"

"Howard, any advertiser with dried bats hangin' in her window is going to get credit from me." Sig heaved a sigh that brought him to his feet, and I walked with him to the water cooler. We carefully measured out small paper cups of water, for Nathan deducted the price of each jug from our salaries. Sig downed his modest draught in a single gulp, then moved on, pulling at the seat of his pants. I meandered over to see Amber in her beauty den, the walls of which were covered with pictures of the new coiffures, the new hemlines, the latest skin care discoveries. "You don't have Blotch Cream here?"

"Blotch Cream?"

"As advertised in the *Midnight Examiner*."

"I never look at the *Examiner,* if I can help it." Amber was clad in a blue tank top, her arms and shoulders bare; her skirt was matching blue, with embroidered eyelets covering it; the bottom three buttons were open, revealing a pair of very pretty knees. I thumbed through her fashion catalogs, at the same time wondering what to do about my own summer clothes, which Crumpacker had so cruelly dismissed. "Amber, I'm taking a survey. What do you think of my wardrobe? Crumpacker has hinted it leaves something to be desired."

"It takes years to develop style, Howard. Some people never do, it's not in their character."

I placed my hand on hers. "You can't possibly know how much I care for you, Amber. I keep your picture beside my bed. The one we used in *My Confession,* remember? I Was Forced To Sell My Body To Support My Habit?"

"You couldn't even see my face in that picture."

"You were never more lovely."

"Siggy injected me in the thigh with a sewing needle attached to an egg timer."

"You have the most beautiful thigh I've ever seen. I have you in an antique frame, bathed in amber light. Should I wake disoriented in the dark, as I so often do, there you are."

"Howard, I have a lunch date in five minutes."

"Amber, if we married, we could have a little home in Tenafly."

"Why in God's name would anyone want to live in Tenafly?" She left for her lunch date, as did the rest of the office, and I returned to my cubicle to muse over some five-by-seven transparencies of young women left by Herr von Germersheim. From their marcelled waves and muscular heft, they appeared to have been members of the Hitler Maiden Bund. Von Germersheim, trying to unload old stock.

A slamming door brought me around in time to see Mitzi Mouse running into the empty office, wearing nothing but a short black kimono, mesh stockings, and high heels. Her war paint was streaked, her hair askew, and she was screaming hysterically, "Guess who I just shot!"

"Shot?"

"I didn't mean to! I pointed it, I was just trying to scare him, but the gun went off." Mitzi's face was white with fear beneath her running mascara. "You know how klutzy I am."

"Who did you shoot?"

"Tony Baloney."

She sank against me, as if trying to hide inside my jacket. I stroked her hair with my hand; it was stiff with hair spray, and on the way to being virtually destroyed. Was Tony Baloney?

"He fell on the floor, clutching his leg. I just wounded him, didn't I?" She looked up at me for reassurance. "Don't let him kill me, Howard."

"Did anyone follow you?"

"I caught a cab right outside the studio." She broke away

from me and went to the window. "There was a black limo behind us, it might've been Tony's." She sank into my chair, clumsily, her kimono opening, revealing the frilly red edges of a garter belt, half undone. "He pulled his gun on me during my coffee break, and that's the only chance I have to work on my poetry. Without my stupid poems —" Tears, running down her cheeks. "— my life is just pornography. It got me crazy. I took out Fernando's pistol, and somehow it went off."

"We've got to call the police."

"Tony Baloney owns the police."

"Mitzi, come this way." I marched her to Nathan's door. He was napping on his couch, hands folded on his stomach, his paunch going up and down as sweetly as a little koala bear's. "Nathan," I said quietly. He opened his eyes. For a moment, he was not of this world, still seeing the rain forests of his dreams.

"Nathan, you remember Mitzi Mouse."

"How you doin'?" Nathan swung his feet off the edge of his couch, yawned, ran a hand over his bald, freckled head.

"Nathan, Mitzi just shot a porno filmmaker named Tony Baloney."

Mitzi interrupted tearfully. "It was a mistake. I was on my coffee break —"

Nathan stared at her. "You shot Tony Baloney?"

"She thinks his torpedoes may have followed her here. Don't you think we should call the police?"

He came off the sofa, took a bottle of poisonous dart sauce from the windowsill. "I just made a fresh batch."

"They're very dangerous," said Mitzi.

"So am I."

"I call them —" Mitzi nervously opened her purse, took out a handful of notepaper with the demented fixation of a bag lady. "— the Hounds of Mordacity."

"They got dogs?"

"Mitzi is given to poetic metaphor, Nathan."

"We got to put the entire staff on alert."

"They're out to lunch."

Nathan looked at his watch. "At this hour? What am I payin' them for?"

"They always wait until you finish your nap."

He punched on his intercom. "Hyacinth, send everybody in here as soon as they come back." He looked up at Mitzi. "Did they know who you was comin' to see in this building?"

"They'd have no way of knowing."

"So they're gonna search the joint." He opened his desk drawer and removed the crossbow pistol.

"Nathan," I said, "this isn't pigeons we're shooting. These are the guys who wiped out the Mastachenza clan in Talerico's Clam House."

"And they're going to wipe me out," sobbed Mitzi.

"We can take them," growled Nathan, hunting lust filling his eyes.

I tried another tack. "Nathan, when a private citizen makes an error of judgment and shoots another private citizen in the leg, the great mechanism of social order must be put in motion. Why don't we just dial 911, which has been established for this purpose?"

"Have you ever tried 911? What social mechanism are you talkin' about? This city is on the verge of chaos. You call an ambulance and what do you get? Bupkis. Little old ladies being beaten over the head with lead pipes dial 911 and die with their asses hangin' out the window. A bunch of vandals are stealin' the roof off a building and the super dials 911 and the next day the whole building's gone and the super's still gettin' a busy signal. 911 is history, Howard. 911 is the opiate of the people."

"Nonsense." I picked up the phone and dialed 911. A recorded announcement said, "All our lines are busy at the moment. The first available operator will attend to your call. Thank you for using 911, and have a nice day." I held the line, listened to the Muzak, and waited. Suddenly, there was a buzzing in my ear and I heard the desperate voice of another private citizen. *"There's a man in my room in his underwear!"*

I waited for the authorities to respond, and then realized she was talking to me. "Hello?"

"He's coming at me!" she shouted.

"Put him on the phone," I said. "I'll handle this."

The next thing I heard was another buzz, and the recorded announcement began again. "All our lines are busy at the moment. The first available . . ."

I stared at the receiver, and slowly hung it up. "Load the blowgun, Nathan."

Nathan began dipping his blow darts into hot sauce. Mitzi picked up the crossbow, there was a metallic *snap* from beside my ear, a gasp from Mitzi, and the arrow bolt of the crossbow was launched just as the door opened. Cardinal Crumpacker went down like a pilgrim at Lourdes, and the bolt whistled over his head, embedding itself in the lobby wall next to Hyacinth, who looked at it in mute horror.

Crumpacker straightened a cuff. "I quit."

Hyacinth came charging in right behind him. "I quit too!" She ran up to Nathan and, squaring off before him, cried, "I tol' you last time, I'm not workin' in no shooting gallery."

"Now listen, both of you," I said, while Nathan continued poisoning his darts, "Mitzi's life is in danger and we've got to help her."

"*I'm* not helping anyone," said Crumpacker. "I'm collecting eighteen weeks of unemployment."

Yvonne came in from lunch, saw the open door and joined us. "What's going on?"

"Somebody's after Mitzi."

"I'm not surprised. Mitzi, dear, you can't expect to go down the street like *that* —"

"She shot Tony Baloney."

"I only wounded him." Mitzi's body sagged, her face went still whiter, and her hands went to her stomach. "I think I'm going to be sick."

"In the wastebasket, dear." Yvonne backed away a few steps, but Mitzi got hold of herself, straightened up. "I'm OK."

"Well, you look awful. Howard, give her something."

"Here, Mitzi, have a mint."

"Whenever I get frightened this happens. Usually it's diarrhea." She was holding her poems in her fist like a wrinkled handkerchief. They were, after all, all she really had, this porno poetess in her kimono and garter belt.

Nathan looked up from his poison. "Cardinal, you see if anyone suspicious is hangin' around the lobby."

"I gave notice two minutes ago." Crumpacker folded his arms in slow, imperious manner.

Mitzi looked at him, eyes pleading.

"Oh, all *right,*" said Crumpacker. "What do they look like?"

"Expensive suits. Heavy jewelry. Mean faces."

"Thanks a *lot.*" Crumpacker, displaying majestic grumpiness, departed the office just as Hattie came in.

I took her slender arm in my hand. "Mitzi's producer interrupted her coffee break, so she shot him."

Hattie brought out her notebook and pencil. "I Told My Boss — One Day You'll Go Too Far."

"And now his hoods are after her. Nathan will give you instructions."

Nathan's bearing had noticeably changed. He was attempting to pull in his paunch, which made his face turn red. "Hattie —" He opened his desk and took out a pair of black razor-edged *Macho Man* throwing stars. "Let me see you use these."

Our confessions editor took one of the stars, wound up, and threw. The ferocious little object hummed through the air and buried itself deeply in the office wall. Hattie looked at us. "I Was A Tomboy But It Didn't Mean I Couldn't Feel Love."

"Take the inner office. If anybody comes through, give 'em the star treatment." Nathan turned to Yvonne. "You watch the fire escape."

"Tony Baloney," said Hip O'Hopp as he entered, "his old man was Big Joe Baloney. The family goes all the way back to Murder Inc. We're screwing around with them?"

"We can't let them blow this kid away," said Nathan. "She come to us for protection, and we're gonna protect her."

Hip sat on the edge of the desk. "Hijacking, heroin, girls,

loan-sharking, you name it, they been in it for three genera-
tions. We did a story on them when I was at the *Times,* and
one of our informants was found in a garbage can in Brooklyn
with his ears cut off."

"Hey," said Nathan, "that don't scare me."

"Did you hear that everyone?" I announced. "It doesn't
scare Nathan."

"Yeah," said Hyacinth, "'cause he's crazy. But I ain't gettin' my ears cut off. Who'd wanna hire a receptionist got no
ears?"

"She has a point, Nathan. How could she handle the
switchboard?"

Nathan looked at Mitzi. "You got your rod?"

"I wish I'd never seen it." Hands still trembling, Mitzi
opened her purse and took out the automatic. We all leaned
sideways a little. Nathan took it, and passed it on to Hyacinth. "Go back to the switchboard." He turned to me. "Go
get more weapons at the sporting goods store. Don't forget
to remind them we get a ten percent discount."

I passed Hyacinth at the reception desk. The pistol was
beside her telephone. She looked up at me. "You know I
could be workin' at Revlon cosmetics?"

I cautiously entered the hall, pressed the elevator button,
got in. The ceiling of our elevator was mirrored, a frivolous
moment in an elevator designer's otherwise subdued career.
The top of my head was now reflected at the floor. I and I,
as the Rasta men say, rode down without incident. I found
Crumpacker at the bookstand in the lobby. He looked up at
me over the pages of *Gentlemen's Quarterly.* "Come along,
Crumpacker. You should be circling the block."

"I should be circling the help wanted ads." He walked with

me across the lobby. We stopped at the door and looked out.

"Crumpacker, we're acting suspiciously. Don't look around, take small animal-like glances left and right."

"*You're* on my right."

"Do you see anyone across the street, there, in the archway of that building, a deranged criminal face."

"That's Siggy."

Siggy dodged through the traffic and joined us on our side of the street, one hand in the seat of his pants. "I lost ten pounds already today, the sweat is running down my leg."

"Sig, just keep walking with us, there's a problem upstairs."

"Uh-oh, the lady with the green ta-tas?"

"Brownsville gangsters."

"That's my old neighborhood. Pitkin Avenue. We'd better keep right on walkin' because those guys put your head in a trash compactor. Or worse."

"Sig, what's worse than having your head put in a trash compactor?"

"Working for Nathan. What'd he do to these guys?"

"He didn't do anything. Mitzi Mouse — you remember Mitzi?"

"Tits out to here?"

"She shot a filmmaker named Baloney."

"Oy gevalt." Siggy vigorously tugged the seat of his pants, as if to get into full battle readiness.

We entered the sporting goods store. "Buy a weapon for yourself, Sig."

"Howard, if that little nafka shot Tony Baloney, the ball game's already over."

I put both my hands to his shoulders, and gazed into his

darting eyes. "Sig, is it the trash compactor you fear?"

"That's right. I don't wanna finish up as a little square package tied with string."

I had a sudden vision of Sig, a perfect cube, with shoes wedged into the bottom and eyes staring out at the top from a flattened head; his hands were at the sides as if holding the box intact. "Sig, Mitzi's in trouble."

"I'll say she is."

"And even Crumpacker, who's been with us less than a week, is on the team." I nodded toward him, and noticed that he'd drifted toward a display of nautical sportswear. "Weapons, Crumpacker, not clothes."

"Clothing is a weapon," he said, but turned toward a tray of fishhooks.

I looked at Siggy, who was edging toward the door. "Sig, old man, Yvonne and Hattie are in the fight. How can you run away?"

"Because I'm a nayfish."

"English please, Sig, if you would."

"A cowardly, weak, pathetic ad salesman."

I turned him toward a shelf of boomerangs. "Arm yourself."

"Oy gevalt." He continued a soft litany of oy-oy-oys, and picked his way through the boomerangs. I selected a baseball bat and helmet and a Swiss army knife. Sig met me at the counter with his boomerang. Crumpacker had a fishing rod and reel. "What are you going to do with that?"

"It happens to be my weapon of choice."

I charged it all, and we left the store, package laden. As we hit the street I noticed, from the corner of my eye, a large black limo moving slowly toward us. "Don't look at it."

"I'm froze like a Popsicle."

"I always look in limos," said Crumpacker. "A certain amount of curiosity is natural." He studied the faint forms behind the sea green glass of the limo. "It seems to be filled with alligators."

The limo passed us and we hurried down the block, beneath a huge construction chute that ran from the top of a building to a dumpster on the street. Clattering down through it was plaster, old lathes, other building debris, and for a moment, as plaster dust filtered down onto us, I had the strangest sensation of being in such a chute myself, struggling along in darkness.

We turned the corner and entered our building, casually chatting, not looking back over our shoulders.

"When I was a kid," said Siggy, "the Baloney brothers beat me up once a week. Now I'm a grown man and they're gonna kill me."

We boarded the elevator and rode upward to our armed camp. "You two go inside, I'm going to check on Yvonne."

I hurried toward the hallway where we'd posted her. She was at the open window, hammering with a sponge mop at a man on the fire escape. He staggered backward on the metal steps, and Yvonne was out the window after him, one of her high heels falling off and her wig twisting sideways. I ran to the sill in time to see the man tumbling down the stairs, a bucket of water emptying on him. He grabbed at the railing, breaking his fall. Yvonne struck him full in the face with his wet mop.

"Maintenance man, Yvonne," I said, before she could drive him from the railing to his death.

"Woikin', lady, I'm woikin' . . ." The fellow swung back

onto firmer footing, soap bubbles coming out of his nose. His shirt and pants were soaked with strong-smelling detergent, and a bit of sponge clung to his ear. "I'm washin' . . . the fuckin' windows . . . see?" He held up his little rubber squeegee.

"Why didn't you identify yourself?"

"A bucket, lady." He yanked it off the stairs and shook it at her. "You think I'm up here takin' a survey?" He grabbed the sponge mop and squeezed it out. "Outta my way, I got to finish."

He climbed on past us, water trailing from his pants legs into his shoes.

Yvonne straightened her wig and climbed back through the window into the hall. She yanked her skirt down. "I loved every minute." She wriggled her foot into her shoe, and worked the heel back and forth until she was securely lodged in the spiked instrument. I left her at her post, and returned to the office. Hyacinth had the Belgian automatic trained on the door as I entered.

"Don't shoot the wrong person," I said as I passed her desk.

"How'm I supposed to know the *right* person?"

"He'll make an aggressive move toward you."

"If I shot every dude made moves on me, be bodies all over town."

I joined the others in the operations room, gave Hip O'Hopp the baseball bat and helmet. "You're our designated hitter."

He slapped the batting helmet onto his head, and tested the weight of the bat in his hand. He cleared his throat, intoned drunkenly: "There was ease in Casey's manner as he stepped into his place . . ." Hip walked away, swaying, bat over his shoulder. Afternoon was not the time of greatest clarity for him, did he even know what we were doing?

Nathan was trying to look in Siggy's shopping bag. "What're you packin'?"

Sig removed his boomerang and Nathan nodded with approval at the exotic hunting implement. "You'll need room to use that effectively."

"Yeah, whyn't I go up to Central Park with it." Sig started for the door.

"You'll cover the roof." Nathan took Sig by the elbow, and pushed him out through the reception room, and the little adman went, boomerang in one hand, seat of his pants in the other. Nathan returned, looked at Crumpacker, who was putting together his fishing rod. "Cardinal, I want you to keep circulating. Hall, staircase, elevators, and back to the reception room. If anybody asks about your pole, tell them you work for *Field and Stream*."

Nathan handed me the crossbow. "OK, so where's the rest of our staff? Why do they take these long lunch hours?"

"Because they're underpaid."

"I gave everyone a bonus this year."

"The apples were deeply appreciated."

Amber entered and Nathan snapped, "Where've you been?"

"In the ladies room."

Nathan never could stand up to Amber. He shuffled his feet for a moment, then: "We've got a company emergency. A gangster is trying to kill Mitzi Mouse."

I handed Amber the crossbow. "And we're sure you wouldn't object to firing this at anyone suspicious who enters the office."

"Suspicious people are always entering the office."

"I beg your pardon?"

"That German person who sells you tit photos."

"Please don't fire a crossbow at Herr von Germersheim, Amber. He's an important supplier."

"I once caught the little Nazi stealing my lunch."

"A mistake, surely."

Amber held the crossbow at arm's length, distastefully. "This is so typical of this office."

Celia Lyndhurst entered, flippers in hand, and we put her in the picture. "You'll cover the hall with the cardinal," said Nathan. "He's out there with a fishin' pole."

Celia was gazing at Mitzi. "We should get her some clothes. What size are you? There's a guy selling hot dresses off a rack on the corner."

"Anything in a nine."

"I'll be back," said Celia, and left us.

"The women in this office," said Nathan, "do whatever they feel like doing." He slung his blowgun and a bandolier of poisoned darts over his shoulder. "Howard, you're in charge of inside operations. I'm going on the roof with Siggy."

Nathan crawled out onto the fire escape. I left his office, and passed Hyacinth at her desk.

"I got a phone call jus' now, and the party hung up right after I answered."

I stared down at her phone set, its contours suddenly resembling the head of an alligator. "Probably a wrong number."

We both knew better. I stepped into the hall. Crumpacker was fishing out the window. He looked at me over his shoulder. "Some suspicious types just walked through down there." He pointed with his pole toward the inner courtyard of the building.

"Resemblance to alligators?"

"Dark suits, very expensive, in dreadful taste."

"Sounds like them."

"What if they saw me fishing out this window?"

"I believe they would be unable to draw any sort of definite conclusion."

I walked down the hall to the art department, but Fernando was nowhere in sight. Gazing up at me from his drawing board was one of Herr von Germersheim's naked Bund Mädchens, standing by a lonely brook, flowers in her blond hair, a dreamy look in her eyes, and three blank lines below her on the layout for me to fill in.

The intercom rang. *We got a man unconscious on the floor out here.*

I raced to the reception area, and found Fernando and Hyacinth standing over a man in a dark suit, who was lying face down with a large lump on the back of his head. A T-square dangled from Fernando's hand.

"He was startin' to speak to me," said Hyacinth, "when Fernando give him one in the head." She put the toe of her shoe under his arm, lifted his elbow. It fell back down heavily.

"Nice work, Fernando. Let's get him out of here." We picked him up and carried him into the hall.

Crumpacker turned from his fishing. "Ralph Lauren tie. Let's see his shoes."

"Crumpacker, old man, if you don't mind —"

Yvonne saw us coming and crawled in through the window. "That's Lorna Lee's lawyer!"

"I give him a good one," said Fernando.

I gazed down at the unconscious lawyer. Young and upwardly mobile. Now downwardly stiff.

"He's been very abusive." Yvonne opened his jacket and, with a gasp of surprise, drew forth a little conceit of the young lawyer's — a silver derringer. "Just what Mother needs."

"We'll take him down the back stairs." I led the way, pushing through the door. "Yvonne, stay at your post."

"But I haven't gone through his other pockets. I should take his charge cards."

We continued down the stairs with the innocent man we'd clubbed comatose. Crumpacker went on ahead to the floor below and nodded us through. We scurried along the hallway to the vacant premises of the former Ajax Exterminating Company, *over 30 years experience, member National Pest Control Association.*

The latch was broken and we pushed inside, into the gloom. A sign on the wall offered free inspection without obligation, any type insect or rodent. We dumped the lawyer behind an abandoned desk.

Fernando opened the desk drawer, brought out an old promotional item of the firm — a large pair of insect antennae, which he attached to the lawyer's brow. They extended a foot off his forehead and ended in two large balls which bobbed gently up and down. I opened the door to the hall, then stepped quickly back: Three goombahs in dark suits were getting off the elevator; they headed toward the rear stairwell.

I waited until they were out of sight, then motioned Crumpacker and Fernando toward the elevator, and pointed upward. They hopped into it, and the doors closed quietly after them. I crept into the stairwell. The strong odor of goombah cologne filled the air.

Yvonne came into view above me, creeping off the windowsill beside the stairwell and pointing her starter's pistol at the backs of the men walking down the hall toward the door of Chameleon Publications.

I pulled out my Swiss army knife, made a random selection, and came up with the bottle opener. It would have to do.

Yvonne called out to them, "Take one more step and I'll fire."

I crept to the top stair and peeked around the edge of the wall. The suavest of the three goombahs had turned and was approaching Yvonne, his manner friendly. "We're looking for Mitzi Mouse. She's a friend of ours. Have you seen her?"

"I'm afraid," I said, stepping into view, "there's some misunderstanding. We're a small religious publisher specializing in Christian tracts. I was just on my way to open a bottle of pop for our hymnal editor." I addressed the suave one in the hopes of negotiating in a civil manner.

"Shuddup, fucknuts." One of the other gentlemen brought his hand out of his pocket. It held a large black revolver. As he pointed it at me I heard, from somewhere down the adjacent hall of the L-shaped corridor, a faint whirring sound. A brightly colored fly landed on the corner of the man's lip. He let out a scream of pain, and was reeled sideways, hooked in the mouth by Cardinal Crumpacker.

The goombah thrashed as he was reeled in, and his gun

fired into the ceiling. Yvonne returned the shot with her derringer and the remaining two goombahs ducked to the floor.
The door to Chameleon Publications opened and Amber
rushed out. Our beauty editor waved her crossbow wildly,
the bowstring snapped with a dreadful twang and a black dot
grew larger before me; I was struck a hammer blow on the
chest. I sprawled backward, gasping for breath, and the bolt
landed with a clang at my feet. I reached into my shirt and
brought out Lady Rana's Lucky Coin Medallion, its face
deeply dented by the fired bolt it had just repelled. Thank
you, Lady Rana, whoever you are. The gangsters were getting to their feet, one of them raising his gun at Amber, but
before he could shoot, a slender dart whizzed through the air
and buried itself in the tip of his nose. Blowgun in hand,
Nathan jumped in off the maintenance scaffold which he'd
lowered to the hall window. Turning back to the nose-pierced
goombah, I saw that his eyes had already glassed over, as
Nathan's hot sauce entered his nervous system. His gun went
off into the floor, and he toppled forward, unconscious.

Hyacinth fired the Belgian automatic from inside the office,
the half-open Chameleon doorway shattering outward in spi-
dering glass. We dropped to the floor and the suave goombah
backed toward the window, the walls of the hallway erupting
in white blossoms of plaster around him. He climbed out onto
the fire escape. I then saw, as if in slow motion, the whirling
trajectory of a boomerang, arcing far out over the city street
and then turning, turning, bearing upon its oval spin a young
Brooklyn boy's long buried prayer of vengeance; by deeply
uttered child magic is it guided, by the ferocity of Jewish
oath is it carried, across the canyon of time and dreams it
comes with increasing velocity, balanced on the genius of the

aboriginal mind, hitting with a loud crack and perfect accuracy right in the middle of the goombah's head, and bringing him down in a heap on the fire escape.

"Pitkin Avenue!" Siggy dropped on him from stairs above, driving both feet into the unconscious gunman's back.

The crook who'd been hooked on the end of Crumpacker's line was racing for the stairs. Crumpacker's pole bent dangerously as line sang free.

Hip O'Hopp, weaving slightly, stepped out from within the stairwell and hit the fellow a tremendous wallop in the kidneys with his baseball bat. The goombah went down with a groan, the line still dangling from his lip. I believe he was a record for goombah taken in that hallway, dressing out at nearly 250 pounds.

We dragged him into the office, and minutes later had him and his two colleagues fastened in handcuffs Melvin used for his *Real Detective* photos. Mitzi Mouse approached cautiously, and Amber and Hattie came behind her, clutching crossbow and throwing stars.

"Of course," said Crumpacker, "my outfit is all *wrong*. I should be wearing something fishy from Abercrombie and Fitch."

Celia entered last, with the clothes she'd just purchased for Mitzi.

"It took you long enough," said Nathan.

"I had to find *shoes* too, you know." She dangled a pair of espadrilles in Nathan's face, and he retreated, while Mitzi wriggled into the outfit Celia'd purchased, a blue-and-white French fisherman's shirt and matching deck pants. Trashy Journalists Save Porno Queen, I Love Them All She Says.

The goombah who'd stopped a dart was waking, the dart

completely through the tip of his nose, like a tribal decoration. His thoughts slowly gathered, dump trucks clanging in the dark. The various contents were emptied, sorted, but when he spoke it was with the voice of a boy of twelve. ". . . I keep all the bubble gum cards, got it? Nobody muscles . . . in . . . on me."

Delirium combined with early aggressive impulses. I'd seen the same thing with Kloss after the hot sauce began circulating in his brain, and the condition worsened within minutes.

". . . Joey play with cap gun, Mama, Joey go bang bang." Regressing still further, the little goombah at play. How had this innocent child, with a strong mother figure in his life, come to be sitting on the floor of a tit publisher with a dart sticking through his nose? The answer awaits the probe of some diligent sociologist.

"Well, whatta we do with these holdupniks now that we've got them?" Siggy, looking down at our prisoners.

Their leader, the soft-spoken one whom Siggy had boomeranged, was now opening his eyes. He discovered his bound hands, saw us standing around him. A con man's smile broke upon his lips. "Look, we've had some serious violence here, but you don't have to keep me tied up, I'm not a wild animal."

"Only animals crap on people's rugs," said Amber.

"What're you talking about?"

"I'm talking about my living room carpet."

"I've never seen your living room carpet."

"A criminal just like you crapped on it and I can't get the stain out."

"Crapping on rugs isn't exactly my style."

"I work hard all day long and when I come home I want to relax, not step in a pile of crap."

"That's right," said Celia, joining in. "We're tired of being victimized."

Hattie grabbed him by the tie and yanked. "My Husband Lost All His Money To The Mob. Now I Have To Take In Laundry."

I drew Nathan and Siggy aside. "We've got to let them go. You understand that."

"They'll just come back," said Siggy. "With machine guns."

"We could keep them tied here," said Nathan. "Feed them dog food once a day."

"Nathan, you've been reading too many *Midnight Examiner*s."

"It's the finest paper in America."

"If you're a yekl." I looked to Siggy, who nodded his approval of my usage of the word.

Yvonne had now joined the other women on our staff and was poking the elegant goombah in the chest with her derringer. "Give me some juicy gangland gossip."

"I'd prefer to start negotiating our release."

Celia took the handsome leader by both ears. "I've got a whole new magazine to fill and I want stories. Hijacking. Loan-sharking. Fixing fights."

"I don't know anything about that. I provide security for Mr. Bulloni."

"Wake the other one up," said Hattie. "I want to hear about All The Young Girls He's Corrupted."

The Four Graces had their notebooks out. It was going to

be a long day for our guests. "Talk," said Amber, flicking the fishing pole.

"Abou' wha' . . . ?" Speech, impaired, owing to hook.

I turned to Nathan. "Well? What are we going to do with them."

"Sell them."

"Who would want to buy them?"

A pensive expression came over our publisher's face and over all our faces, as we realized it wasn't easy to dispose of three able-bodied killers. Then Siggy spoke up. "We'll put them in the deep freeze."

"Siggy, this is not a frozen food item, three for a dollar. These are human beings."

"I'm talking deep hypnotic trance. We'll take them over to Madame Veronique of Voodoo Afrique."

"Come on, Siggy, I can't accept that."

"Listen, Howard, if she feels like it, Madame Veronique could make these guys think they're bullfrogs. Or French ticklers. Or frigging hot dogs."

"*I'm* for the French tickler," said Hattie.

I kept silent about Hattie's preference, but I'd certainly expected more from the editor of *Young Brides Tell All*. The decision, in any case, was Nathan's. I turned to him. "Well?"

"Will she take all three of these gumheads?"

"She might," said Siggy, "but it's gonna cost us."

"How much?"

"She's into us for five g's already. She might want us to waive it."

"We'll negotiate."

We lifted the three hoodlums to their feet, with Amber,

Celia, Hattie, and Yvonne still pecking away with their questions. The handsome goombah was trying to get to Amber. "It's all been a misunderstanding. Tell your friends that, will you? We wanted to see if Mitzi was all right. Her gun went off accidentally, we know that. She's the star of our film, we need her."

"Then why did you pull out guns?"

"Look, let me introduce myself. My name is Angelo Sabella, I've got two tickets tonight for the Met. Pavarotti is singing. Let me take you to supper first and then we'll go hear the most beautiful voice in the world."

"Don't listen to him," said Hattie. "His Whispered Promises Will Come To Nothing In The End."

I drew Siggy aside. "How are we going to get them through the main lobby?"

"Whyn't we take them down on that?" Siggy nodded through our shot-up door toward the window in the hall, where the scaffolding still hung. "We'll look like the building inspectors."

"Hyacinth, call a limo service and have them in the vacant lot below in fifteen minutes."

"Wait a second," said Amber. "That man wants to take me to the opera."

"I regret to say, Amber darling, Angelo is on the way to be turned into a bullfrog by a voodoo sorceress."

"I haven't been anywhere in weeks."

"He came here to kidnap poor Mitzi."

"That's entirely between them, and has nothing to do with our relationship."

"A minute ago you were accusing him of crapping on your rug."

"We've established rapport now." She straightened the webbed blue belt that circled her waist, and struck what I felt was an attitude.

"Amber, he's going to be busy for a while."

"Doing what?"

"Eating flies, if all goes according to plan."

"Limo be here in ten," announced Hyacinth.

We shoved our prisoners out into the hall, their wrists still handcuffed. The one with a dart in his nose was feeling it tenderly with his fingertips, as he recited a nursery rhyme he'd learned as a little goombah. "Who killed Cock Robin? I said the Sparrow, with my bow and arrow . . ."

We pushed them toward the open window. Siggy climbed out and steadied the scaffold. I prodded our prisoners. "After you."

"You're pushing this too far, my friend," said Angelo, turning his cold charm on me. "You're way out past where a person like you should be."

Yvonne leaned her head out the window. "Darling, be careful."

"Don't worry, Yvonne, we're only lowering ourselves in a dangerously overweighted scaffold." I nodded to Siggy and Crumpacker, and they released the catches on the pulleys. We began our descent.

The aluminum scaffold rocked and swayed disagreeably in the hot summer air, and suave Angelo kept working on my confidence. "Listen, I'm not vengeful. I'll smooth things out for you. The family will reward your cooperation."

"Angelo, tell him to take thith futhin' fith-hook outta my mouth . . ."

We descended slowly past the windows of the Ajax Exterminating Company, Any Type Insect or Rodent. On the floor, Lorna Lee's lawyer was just coming to consciousness and discovering the antennae Fernando had fastened to his brow, the expression on his face much like that of Kafka's commercial traveler who wakes up as a cockroach one morning.

I gazed at the vacant lot below. Rubble was strewn about much of it, through which moved several rodents the Ajax Exterminating Company had failed to suppress. Turning my head I could see along the canyon of the street to the Hudson River sparkling in the distance. Siggy sent the ropes through the pulleys, letting us down in little jerks. A pistol stuck out of one pocket, a boomerang out of the other. Sweat ran down his forehead, and he grunted with each length of rope. He looked at me. "Why ride in a crowded elevator?"

We lowered past an open window where a secretary was taking the air. Crumpacker tipped his fish pole politely. And so we descended, through light and shadow, the building across the way blocking the sun from the lower half of ours; a shadow crossed Siggy's suit, then Crumpacker's, then spilled over our faces. Lowering into the cooler depths with our prisoners, I felt the great cauldron in which we stew, in which we turn, stirred by Mr. Blotch Cream, who is slowly boiling us down.

The scaffold touched the ground. Broken bottles sparkled in the sunlight. Graffiti covered the walls. We crawled off onto the blazing dust, just as the Aswan Limo Service entered the lot — a battered station wagon that rolled over the carpet of broken glass and pulled up beside us. A Middle Eastern driver looked out at us, a cigarette dangling from his lips. "You want for ride?"

Angelo was making difficulties, planting himself stubbornly in the sand. Siggy hit him over the head with his boomerang, and the elegant goombah fell toward the car door. Our driver blinked at this but withheld comment. Siggy shoved Angelo into the back of the limo, and Crumpacker lifted his pole; the hooked goombah went on tiptoe, quietly, into the station wagon. Our driver blinked again, and turned to watch as Crumpacker reeled the goombah up straight in his seat. Then the last of our prisoners, dart still in his nose, settled in. Siggy climbed onto a swivel jump seat fastened to the floor in the rear, facing our captives. I crawled in front beside the driver, and slipped him a twenty-dollar bill.

"Siggy, give him the address."

"We're goin' up to a Hundred-tenth and Broadway."

The driver looked at Siggy, then me, then the twenty, and reaching some kind of decision, put the station wagon in gear. I looked at his hack license dangling from the dash.

UQAL MUSSA

He swung out into the street, sneaking glances into the rearview mirror, at one passenger with a fishhook in his lip and another with a dart through his nose. His head twitched my way again, and he began chattering nervously as he steered us up the avenue. "Some days no traffic, you fly, making money. Other times, not so good." Eyes up to mirror, checking fishhook, back to street. "I didn't expect so much passenger today. I can see from here people standing waiting for cab." Back up to mirror and the nose dart. "I pass already ten."

"I suppose you're wondering," I said, "why one of your passengers has a fishhook in his lip."

"I have learn is good explanation for everything." He found a break in traffic and scooted forward, fist on the horn. His cigarette smelled like burning cardboard, and he wore a garish Hawaiian shirt with bright red slacks, and a New York Yankees baseball cap. His shiny loafers had little leather tassels on them and a gold chain hung around his neck. "I come here ten year ago from Egypt. You ever been the Middle East? The secret detectives there works more better than any other country in the world." He turned toward me, his glance asking were *we* secret detectives?

Crumpacker spoiled the illusion, I think, by turning cranky at that moment. "I'm going *straight* home when we're done with this."

"Of course, Crumpacker."

"And I *don't* expect this kind of nonsense tomorrow."

"We're not in control of tomorrow, Crumpacker. We take what fate brings us. You, as editor of *Prophecy* magazine, should understand that better than anyone."

Angelo was waking from his most recent boomeranging. He looked at Siggy, and his voice had lost its civilized edge. "You'll get yours, shorty."

"You used to beat the shit out of me on Pitkin Avenue," said Siggy. "I was the puny pitseleh down the block."

"When I'm kicking your face in one of these days maybe I'll remember."

Uqal Mussa's eyes were riveted on the rearview mirror, and his hand went under the dash, where it tentatively fondled the handle of a nightstick. "It's all right," I said quietly. "The situation is under control."

He withdrew his hand from the nightstick, and looked at me, his childlike gaze troubled by doubts. I answered him as best I could. "The man in back with the fish pole is a minister."

Uqal Mussa blinked, as this information slowly passed through the translation barrier. "Man of cloth?"

"That's right, Mussa. A clergyman."

"Ah, now I see," he said, nodding his head. "I pick up clergyman once befores."

"The last thing they wish is violence, you understand."

"Sure, sure, they come to New York on visit, first ask me where is Umpire State Building, then where is topless show, I take them to the Metropole." We were passing through Times Square at the moment and, as we passed the Metropole, Mussa pointed it out to Crumpacker. "You go dere, Fodder. You like fine."

"Thank you so much."

"Don't mention, I know what clergyman want. You hungry, gentlemans? I take you place have cabbages like grape leaves and the squash with the seeds out and fill it with rice, ground meat. And —" He nodded in the rearview mirror toward Crumpacker. "— they got women dance with jewel in belly button for Fodder."

"I can't wait, I'm sure."

"You eat something, everybody be more friendly." Uqal Mussa glanced into his rearview mirror again, his gaze still apprehensive about what he saw in back: Siggy's pointed revolver, our bound prisoners, the dart, the fishhook. I stuffed another twenty-dollar bill in his ashtray and said quietly, "You're going to make money today."

He pocketed the twenty. "Is only for my family. You understand?"

"Perfectly."

"I have small daughter, sir. She need her fodder." He pointed to a framed photograph on his dash. "Born in America. All the opportunities." He looked at me, a plea in his eyes. "If her fodder die, where she be?" Saying which, he executed a maniacal lane-hopping maneuver across the flow of uptown traffic, causing a flurry of angry shouts from short-fused cabbies much more likely to kill him than I was, but he was ahead of the snarl now and moving fast. We continued along uptown, Mussa pointing out various Middle Eastern eating establishments, and topless bars for Crumpacker. All the while, Siggy sat hunched in the jump seat, pistol pointed at our captives. Angelo was trying a different tactic with him now, his voice once again silky. "So you grew up in the neighborhood. You've come a long way. You can go a lot further if you cooperate."

"I been waitin' years for this moment," said Siggy.

"My employer will pay you for Mitzi Mouse."

"I don't sell my friends down the river."

"Mitzi's just a cheap little bimbo."

"That's how I like them."

Traffic eased as we passed Columbus Circle, and Uqal Mussa sped on through the Upper West Side. We passed the bars, movie theaters, and restaurants which had been my life, more or less, and now I was speeding by with three bound prisoners, one of whom had a dart in his nose. I'd become a vigilante, had taken the law into my own hands, and was passing my laundry, where Mrs. Shivitz at this moment was destroying my shirts. Mussa, reminiscing:

"I have been back home to Egypt last December. When I left was something, when I returned was something else."

"To be expected."

"Every country has his certain things."

"Absolutely."

"Here, I adapt myself. They do many things different, I watch, I learn."

"This is the place," said Siggy.

Mussa stopped the limo in front of an old apartment building on upper Broadway. He reached under the dash. "I bring mace can, extra-special service."

We eased our prisoners across the sidewalk, Crumpacker keeping his fish pole low, Siggy pressing his weapon through the cloth of his jacket into Angelo's back. The dart in Joey's nose drew a few glances, but New Yorkers practice tolerance, and a moment later we had our captives in the hallway of the building. An elderly woman was coming down the stairs. She looked at our prisoners.

"I don't know nuttin'." She shuffled on by.

"Hey lady," said Angelo, "we've been abducted."

"I ain't seen a ting." She pushed past us into the street, the door swinging closed behind her. Siggy took out his pistol, pointed. "Up."

"You've been lucky," said Angelo. "But you're going to start getting unlucky."

Crumpacker lifted his fish pole sharply.

"For Chrith thake, Angelo, shut upth, it geth the fitherman pithed."

We mounted the stairs. It was one of those charming upper Broadway buildings, walls painted in durable institutional green and decorated by a web of demented oaths scratched with a sharp tool. Uqal Mussa was feeling more comfortable with the situation. "You give me another twenty dollar, I wash the stairs."

"Why do you want to wash the stairs?"

"I wash, see nobody come bother you."

"Ah, *watch* the stairs."

"Yeah, wash good."

"Just come along with us and wash those three gentlemen." I pointed at our prisoners and then handed him the twenty, which he took with a nod, your humble immigrant, adapting.

"Here we are," said Siggy, as we reached the second floor. He knocked on the door of Voodoo Afrique and entered. I prodded our prisoners in ahead of us. A heavy scent of burnt herbs filled the air, and a spidery-limbed old black man was seated at a table filling orders, a stack of mailing cartons before him, along with a shelf of various tinctures, powders, animal extremities, and potions. He looked up at Siggy. "How y'doin'," he said in a soft purr. He did not comment or even seem to notice Siggy's pistol, but he took note of Crumpacker's fly rod. "Been doin' some fishin'."

"Yes," said Crumpacker. "I just have a mad urge sometimes."

"I like a little fishin' myself." The old man taped shut a parcel. "Get out in the sunshine, get some fresh air. Do a man good." He glanced at Crumpacker's dangling goombah, then began filling another box. "Pack a nice lunch, go off to one of the piers, fish all day. Don't care if I catch somethin'."

"No," said Crumpacker, "neither do I."

"What you use fo' bait, if you don't mind my askin'?"

"One of those feathery things on a hook."

The elderly assistant glanced again at Crumpacker's catch, whose lip sported the bright, winged edges of a tied fly. "Yes, so it is, didn't see it at first. You like that kind of bait?"

"I never use anything else."

"You stick with what works."

"That's right."

"Yes, that's the best. I mean, if it works for you, that's all that matters." He turned toward Siggy. "Madame V's in back, you kin go right in."

Siggy led us to the back of the store, and drew aside a curtain. Prodding our captives along, we stepped into Madame Veronique's cavern of voodoo dreams, where she lay fanning herself on a gaudily tufted couch, with a pitcher of iced coffee beside her on a small wooden table whose legs were carved cobras, hoods spread. Her corpulent form was draped in a tentlike dress; her coffee-colored complexion was like a young girl's, but she was a woman in her fifties. A soap opera was playing on her TV. She raised her hand imperiously. We kept silent until the commercial, then Siggy said, "I got some business for you."

Her eyes didn't leave the TV set. "How much you got to spend?"

"We'll make a deal."

She touched her remote control unit and the sound of the TV commercial was mercifully lowered. Madame Veronique swung her legs off the couch and planted her sandaled feet firmly on the floor. "My ankles swell up in this weather."

"Are you getting enough potassium?" I asked, a problem Dr. Husbands had touched on in a recent column. "You should have a banana a day, with lots of green leafy vegetables."

"Talk on."

"I also suggest supplementing with all the B vitamins, especially B_6."

"They give me a devil of a time," she said, gently rocking back and forth on them, the soles of her thick sandals squeaking. Much as I sympathized, if she couldn't cure her own swollen ankles, she couldn't be much of a voodoo queen, and now we'd have to dump these goombahs in Tenafly, in their underwear, quickly.

"Well, Madame Veronique, I hope your circulation improves, and now we must be going. Siggy can get you a good buy on vitamins."

Siggy stepped in front of me, and spoke quietly to her. "Madame V, we need to get those three pricks off our back. Give them a bad case of amnesia, like you gave me when I forgot to collect any dough from you for six months. Except with them, make it like for ten years or so. Make 'em forget what's goin' on."

"I make them forget they were born." Madame V chuckled as her glance fell on the goombahs. "I make them itch all over."

"OK, throw in the itch too."

"I see my ad running full-page for the same ten years to come and never no bill collector arrives here."

I pulled Siggy aside. "Nathan isn't going to like it, Sig. This woman has no more power than Dr. Husbands."

"She gave me amnesia for six friggin' months."

"Something else must have caused it."

"Yeah, what?"

"Nu-Age Wrinkle Remover, for one, or any of the other toxic substances you deal with on a daily basis, but not from something this woman concocted. Sig, she sells monkey hair mail order, and that's about it."

"She's all we've got."

Madame Veronique stepped over to us, peered into my face. Her bones were strong, here eyes deep-set and large, a remarkably handsome woman. Her face came still closer to mine as she asked, "You're a doctor?"

"I'm a doctor like you're a doctor."

"Sometimes my heart skips a beat."

"Mild arrhythmia."

"It scares the life out of me."

"Have you tried going off coffee?"

"Madame V," said Siggy, nodding toward the goombahs, "you take care of them, we'll take care of your ad."

"I will put their heads in a cloud. Should I touch their *calabash* as well?"

"Hey, be my guest."

"If I touch their *calabash* they will be idiots for seven eternities."

"That sounds about right, don't it, Howard?"

Angelo called to Madame V. "Whatever they're paying you, I'll double it. Let's put the hex on them."

Madame Veronique turned to Siggy. "My services being bid on, magazine man."

"Siggy," I whispered, "we've got to get out of here before this woman learns any more about us. She's fully capable of blackmailing the firm."

"Madame V," said Siggy, "how would you like a double-page spread every week?"

"In color."

"As much color as we got." Sig gestured to a shelf filled with pickled toads and dried bird claws. "Let's get started."

She opened a copy of the *Midnight Examiner* that lay on her coffee table, and pointed to the photograph of her face, looking up out of her ad. "You touch up my photo, make me look like Joan Collins?"

"We got an airbrush man on the premises who can do anything. He works mainly coverin' nipples, but —"

"My nipples already covered. Ain't nobody going to mess with them." She turned toward our hostages. "I'll take care of these *malfacteurs*." Snake bracelets rattled on her wrist as she waved a long index finger at them. How had Siggy, a modern, aggressive ad salesman, fallen for this act? Madame V's voice went into a gospel singsong as she stepped closer to the gunmen. "A cloud will enter their skull. No living man will be able to wake them to their former life. They will wander the earth like Adam."

Angelo gazed anxiously at Madame Veronique. "Just name your price."

"It has been named," said Madame V. "It has been answered."

"Ten g's, delivered in an hour."

"You cannot deliver Joan Collins, nor the full-page color spread. Fate has not put such power in your hands, and so you are going to reap hard luck. All belongs to the night and the Djab."

Uqal Mussa removed his Yankees cap, and bowed religiously.

Madame Veronique stepped in front of the hooked crook, looked him up and down; she opened a jeweled snuffbox, snapped her fingers by his nose, and the fellow fell in a heap on the floor, a few grains of a sandy powder remaining on his cheek.

"Don't come near me with that shit!" Angelo was backing toward the door. Madame V's elderly assistant jabbed him from behind with a rhinoceros horn, and Madame V snapped her fingers by Angelo's nose. He spun slowly around. His eyes had the look of a dead jellyfish. He opened his mouth to speak; a sigh came out, and he too sank to the floor. Our hostess approached Joey, the last of the prisoners, who sat docilely, a dart in his nose, Nathan's concoction in his brain, and a child's trusting look in his eyes. Madame Veronique pulled one of his lids down and examined the white of his eye. With equal interest did she study the dart embedded in his nose. She drew it carefully out; her eyes closed, her nostrils flared. "A deep, fine poison."

"I think it was just Jambalaya Jubilee Hot Sauce, Madame V," said Siggy.

Madame Veronique gave him an indulgent smile, and then dropped the dart into a jar, which she quickly sealed. "It will cook in there, and its demon age nicely." She turned back to Joey, pulled out his tongue. "Observe the color — white as a snail." She turned to me. "No other herb doctor has the full-page ad arrangement with you?"

"No, certainly not. My colleague here, Cardinal Crumpacker, can back me up on that. He heads our religious section."

Madame Veronique's expression changed radically as she turned toward Crumpacker. "The ship of faith shines on the holy seas."

Not wishing her dusting powder anywhere near my calabash, I was inching slowly away from her, but she seemed to care little for me, it was Crumpacker who had her attention. Her face was only inches from his, and she was nodding her head slowly up and down.

"He is the fisherman. He hooks men's souls. I have spoken."

Uqal Mussa put his Yankees cap back on and tugged at the peak. "He is man of cloth, I take everyone the Metropole no charge, but please don't put powder my nose, I have large family and big plans."

"This one," said Madame Veronique, looking at Uqal, "is also at the magazine?"

"He's a hired chauffeur."

"We go to Bloomingdale's." She strode majestically into the reception room, and we followed. Her elderly assistant was seated again at his table, filling monkey hair orders. He looked up at her as we passed. "The other three gentlemens are stayin' with us?"

"They shall not move for many lifetimes."

"Won't bother me at all."

Madame Veronique slung a pocketbook over her shoulder and we left her establishment, descending the stairs single file behind her to the lobby, and out into the sweltering wave of heat radiating from the pavement. "This hot weather drag me down something awful," she said, and turned to me as we crossed toward the station wagon. "I know what you're going to tell me, doctor man."

"You've got to lose fifty pounds."

"A half gallon of ice cream is what I like." She slid into the back seat of the station wagon, her skirt rising upward and providing me with a view of her massive thighs. She caught my glance. "You have seen the truth, magazine man."

"And hoping it will save me, Madame V." I settled in beside her as Crumpacker came in the other door, fishing pole in hand. She lifted his dangling hookless line on her finger. "His bait is gone, but still he fishes. That is faith."

Her warm body was pressed against mine; she was a Big

Womans. "We shall shop and prosper." She looked at me with her large, dark eyes. "You'll put me on a reducing program."

"Dr. Husbands's Thirty Day Wonder Diet requires a certain amount of willpower."

"I got none at all," said Madame V, opening her purse and taking out a flowered tin of hard candies, several of which she popped in her mouth. "A woman my age can get lonely, and then I go for pizza with extra cheese and a six-pack."

"Not a perfect solution, Madame Veronique, if you'll forgive my saying so."

She turned toward Crumpacker, looked him up and down. "I like holy men." She wound his fishing line around her finger.

"I've had a long day," said Crumpacker.

Madame V ran a luminous silver fingernail down his cheek. "I'll give you something make you jump like a jackrabbit."

"I've heard *that* before."

Uqal, steering through traffic, spoke over his shoulder to Madame Veronique. "Clergymans got to have special floor show."

"Drive on, driver."

"Am driving on."

"You're a slim-jim," said Madame Veronique, leaning back away from Crumpacker, to take him all in.

"I need a cold shower, I'm feeling cranky."

"Lord, I know how you feel." Madame V took out a bamboo fan and started working it back and forth across her face. "When the city gets like this, my legs feel like two hot sausages ready to split."

"It's been one thing after another all day."

"All belongs to Djab."

"And I'm certainly not up for Bloomingdale's. I have to be in the *mood*."

"My rent is due, and there's no good men my age around." Madame V snapped her fan closed, looked toward the street. "Sometimes I think I go back to Port-au-Prince."

Uqal Mussa made an insane turn across traffic, and Madame Veronique heaved against Crumpacker. Her hand fell upon his knee, and when she pulled it away, a strange damp palm print covered his pants leg. Crumpacker looked down at it in horror, then turned to Madame V. "Do you *mind*?"

"It is the *liquide astral*. It leaks from my hand, from all my foolishness with hoodoo."

Crumpacker patted frantically at it with his handkerchief. "Does it stain?"

"It can never be removed."

"Well, isn't *that* wonderful." Crumpacker stared in dismay at his pants leg.

"Fortune can be read from the pattern there. I see a big black dog charging at you."

"Oh, that's just Woman Gives Birth To Puppies," said Crumpacker, turning crotchety.

"You will not stop this dog with a salami."

"Am I looking at a dye job here?"

"The Djab never lie."

"The fabric will never be the same, of course."

"I have given you warning."

"And I have an outfit I'll never wear again." Crumpacker was in a huff now. I'd been hoping to avoid this, but how could I have anticipated supernatural moisture on his pants?

He would take considerable cheering up which, as his editorial director, I felt obliged to attempt.

"Bloomingdale's, Crumpacker. Pants replacement. Steady on."

"You don't just *buy* a pair of pants."

"Some sort of preparation required?"

"I wouldn't expect you to understand."

Siggy turned around toward Crumpacker. "I buy all my clothes on Orchard Street."

"They look it."

"Shlomo's Designer Fashions and Knitwear."

"Please don't go on."

"Shlomo knows clothing." Siggy turned toward the front once more, satisfied with this modest defense. His suits, as noted previously, were designed with the seat material permanently inserted up his buttocks.

I noticed with alarm that Uqal Mussa was once again preparing for a turn completely across traffic, jaw set. Before I could protest, he'd made his move. Brakes screeched in back and in front of us, horns blared, and Mussa's hand remained steady on the wheel, his other hand out the window, middle finger in the air, his only form of directional signal.

"I cannot take all this shaking up." Madame Veronique, righting herself after pitching across my lap. "When I was twenty I went for wild rides, but then I was slender. A young girl takes a lot of bounces." She opened her fan again, and waved it across her face. "Rent due, and going gray. I don't mind in winter so much, but summer gets me down."

On we plunged, bound for Bloomingdale's; the streets were filled with others upon similar errand, shopping for that precious bauble, that perfect ensemble, that will-o'-the-wisp that will tell us who we are. And if after purchase, there is still uncertainty about identity, well, that is what the *Midnight Examiner* is for, read all about it, Man Marries Orangutan In Quiet Ceremony, I Love Her Says Groom Even Though She's Hairy.

Madame Veronique picked up the hem of her dress, flapped it back and forth to fan her legs. "I need a big air conditioner in my place. You make me rich, yes?"

"Large-scale national advertising on a regular basis will enhance your reputation, Madame Veronique. Whether it will make you rich is something only the Djab can know for sure."

"I could do big business if the FDA weren't always after me. Those boys don't want hoodoo power in the mails."

"The public must be protected, Madame V. Siggy here can tell you about a woman's green ta-tas."

Mussa's countenance was set into a determined frown; we had become hopelessly snarled in traffic; he spied an opening, the wheel spun in his hand and we went *up on the sidewalk.* Pedestrians flung themselves into doorways; the support pole of a bakery awning collapsed across our windshield, temporarily blinding Mussa, but he recovered nicely and, head out the window, turned at the corner into a side street, where he sped away, Siggy tossing the dangling awning behind us.

"Driver, what in hell's wrong with you?" Madame Veronique, righting herself again. "Did somebody slip you a wanga?"

"Where you go they say New Yorker drivers the most crazy in the world. Is not true. But by the time you don't feel it."

Madame Veronique shook her head, exasperatedly, and

picked up the edge of her dress again. "You magazine men move too fast for this fat hoodoo woman."

"Bloomingdale's just ahead, madame," said Mussa. "Perfect parking spot." He arrowed our vehicle into a torn-up patch of pavement, in which two Con Ed men were working, thick electric cables at their feet and Mussa's bumper behind them. They turned around angrily, and one of them gestured with his thumb back toward the traffic.

Madame Veronique nudged Crumpacker. "Everybody out. We must get my dress for the full-color ad."

We stepped into the exposed earth, and the Con Ed workers turned toward us. "Whattya, nuts? Move that car!"

"Come here, hardhat," said Madame V, beckoning toward the black member of the Con Ed team. The pieces of torn-up pavement were obviously giving her swollen feet some trouble, for she had to lean on the fender of the car. The man walked toward her impatiently, his tool belt creaking. "Look here," he said, but Madame Veronique interrupted, saying, "No, you look *here*," and opened her eyes wide, false eyelashes fluttering like the legs of a tarantula. "I am a bone woman. Do you want to spend the rest of your life in a tree, playin' with your dingdong like a chimp?"

He backed off, but his angry colleague stepped forward. "Hey, what the Christ — lookit this fuckin' car —"

The black Con Edder spoke softly in the other one's ear, and that puzzled fellow turned back toward us now, brow furrowed; he looked at the hobbling fat lady with irritation but was taking no chances. The underground was vast, the problems of the cables endless, and those few lines exposed at his feet could wait while a bone woman shopped.

Crumpacker's élan vital returned, his system galvanized by

the sight of Bloomie's. Madame Veronique put her arm through his, and they headed for the entrance, while I remained with Mussa and Siggy on the curb. "Mussa, I'd like you to write two hundred and fifty words on Defensive Driving for *Ladies Own Monthly,* which as you may know, is a leader in its field."

"Can't write the English."

"Not strictly necessary."

"Only way we can do, secretary sit at typewriter, I flog her."

"Fine, fine, only we call it dictating, Mussa, not flogging."

"Car is weapon, that's how you do. Use like weapon, nobody get in the way then you turn. Not all of them they like to punish or kill or do wrong things."

He had the feel of the thing, I felt, a remarkable story was in the making. Traffic flowed past, the Con Ed men struggled with their cables, and the summer sun shone faintly through the pollution layer onto the city's gleaming windows; Siggy was staring upward, while thoughtfully picking at the seat of his pants. "I got a client on this block. Prime Time Pimple Salve. I'm owed dough by the sonofabitch. I'm owed dough by everybody. Nobody pays their bills anymore."

"You owed money," said Mussa, "we collect." He opened the trunk of his cab and took out a tire iron. "Where we go?"

Siggy led the way across the street. I remained with the car, leaning against its fender. "You have any idea how long the bone lady gon' be?" The Con Ed worker, at a respectful distance.

"She's shopping for a dress."

He turned to his colleague. "We might as well go and have some coffee."

"We oughta call the motherfuckin' cops is what we should do."

"Sure, they haul her car away, and tonight my dick fall off." He hung his CONSERVE ENERGY sign on the trunk of our car, and tipped his hardhat back. "We goin' to get coffee."

Needing a pick-me-up myself, I swallowed a caffeine tablet and presently my body was back to its normal level of functioning, heralded by the breaking of a small blood vessel in my nose. My heart was hammering in my chest, by which, along with my bleeding nose, I knew I was now at my point of maximum alertness. At my feet were the jagged nerve ends of the city, thick strands of cable leading god-knows-where, to facilitate the lives and businesses of decent men and women, as well as cheats, thieves, and fiends, all pottering around somewhere at this very moment, their plans and my own faintly connected, like the threaded cables below, the city one great brain whose thoughts were always haywire.

How long did I stand there, with soul adrift in the void, waiting? See the *Midnight Examiner* for details.

Siggy and Mussa came across the street, Siggy's step lively, signifying commission earned, and Mussa's tire iron tipped with Prime Time Pimple Salve.

"We've shopped like great beings," said the voice of Madame V from behind me. Turning, I saw her holding up packages in both hands. "Ready for full-color, magazine man."

Mussa opened the trunk and stowed the packages, after which he held the back door for Madame V. Crumpacker and I settled down on either side of her once again, and we shot back out into traffic.

"This holy editor has the true eye," said Madame V. "He

has clothed me wisely." She handed the bill to me.

"I see you spared no expense, Crumpacker."

"He shops with flare. I am deeply moved."

Mussa gave his regular directional signal, finger up, and screeched across traffic, horns blaring at him from every side. The tortuous paths through Manhattan are trod by millions of pilgrims, raving, praying, hallucinating, dreaming of deliverance; had we all the glowing abdomen of fireflies and could we be photographed from above, what exquisite weaves would be seen. We bounced into the vacant lot beside the Chameleon offices. "Whole damn city, five minutes." Mussa tapped his watch.

"A remarkable achievement, Mussa."

"Where my secretary? I flog her now."

"Madame Veronique, there may be other gunmen waiting for us in the building. We'd be safer ascending on the scaffold."

We took our places around her and, with Mussa and Siggy manning the hoist ropes, began our ascent. The afternoon sun slanted through the canyons, turning the windows a faint gold. Mussa breathed heavily as he pulled on the rope. "Getting blister on the plams." He held up one of his dark hands. Madame Veronique ran a fingernail along a crease in Mussa's plam. "Lifeline like an elephant." She folded his fingers inward. "This one is hard to kill."

Crumpacker fished off the center of the scaffolding, in an introspective attitude. What might he catch in the bright golden air of late afternoon? He jerks his hookless line, he reels in, he casts again.

We hoisted ourselves on up to the roof, fixed the scaffolding, and helped Madame Veronique over the edge, our feet sinking slightly into the roof's soft black skin. Ventilators turned lazily in the gentle rooftop breeze, and we could see far downtown, where the towers of trade and finance blazed with reflected light, Mr. Blotch Cream's great copper cauldron cooking.

Siggy went down the stairs first, gun out, then waved us after him. We plunged into the Chameleon offices, where Hyacinth greeted us. "'Bout time you come back," she said in her bossy way, but when her eyes met Madame Veronique's, she quickly shut up.

"Such a pretty girl," said Madame V. "Has love been good to you?"

"Not lately, it ain't."

"I'll give you a *poudre* for your man friend's coffee. It will change his attitude sharply."

"Only thing change him is a gunshot in the hip."

Madame V turned to me. "I make good strong love potions for others, but on me they always fail, and I don't know why."

I led her to Nathan's office door. He was stirring a container of his Jambalaya Jubilee Hot Sauce as we entered, his darts laid neatly out on the desk before him.

"Mission accomplished, Nathan. I should like to introduce you to Madame Veronique, a specialist in psychopharmacology and one of our most distinguished advertisers. In exchange for her help in protecting our offices, we're running Madame Veronique's ads without charge in the *Midnight Examiner*."

"Nobody gets free ads in my publications."

Madame Veronique opened her purse and took out a dried monkey claw. I waited with eager anticipation; in a few seconds, Nathan would be rolling around on the floor in a hypnagogic trance.

Madame V stood and moved behind my chair. I felt the little nails of the monkey claw run through my hair. My head jerked back as if yanked by a string, and I saw the ceiling spinning around; I fell backward, a peculiar barnyard sound issuing from my throat, and then I was on all fours, barking like a baboon. Nathan's chuckling came as if from a great distance, and I scurried under his desk, pawing at my genitals, which seemed just at the moment rather brightly colored.

"All right," said Nathan. "You get the ads. But I get to see Howard like this once a week."

Madame V reached under the desk and stroked my forehead, releasing me from the spell. I crawled out, scratching vaguely.

Madame Veronique moved to the door. "I shall now pose for the double-page spread."

I held the door for her as she left, not without the lingering feeling that I had bright red callosities on my buttocks and a thinly haired tail of moderate length.

"We ain't seen the last of Tony Baloney," said Nathan.

"Madame Veronique will take care of it," I said, sitting on my vivid callosities.

"Keep her ads small."

"She's getting little argument from me, Nathan, on any subject." I continued to make room on my chair for a tail.

"When their three goons don't show, they'll come lookin'. I figure tomorrow morning."

"What do we do with Mitzi?"

"She should stay in the office for the night because her

own place'll get knocked off. Fernando can stay here and guard her."

I saluted and returned to my office. Madame Veronique was at my desk reading a copy of *Young Nurse Romance.* "Where is my photographer?"

"Madame V, I wonder if I might have my desk back? We'll just find you a quiet spot —"

"I'm too hot and tired to get up again." The monkey claw was on my desk.

"Fine, no problem at all, I'll just go and finish my work out in the hall, it'll be perfectly convenient." I scooped up my layouts and left my cubicle, but was stopped by Amber. "What did you do with that beautiful opera lover?"

"He was a professional hit man."

"He invited me to dinner."

"He will not be keeping the engagement."

She looked at me from beneath expertly shaded eyelids. "I'm not getting any younger."

"We here at Chameleon Publications love and respect you. As your editor in chief, I am about to embrace you." And I did.

To my great surprise, she laid her cheek wearily against my chest. "Oh, Howard, I don't know why I'm feeling so cross."

"Let me cook you supper."

She raised her head, looked over my shoulder. "Who is that woman smoking a cigar in your office?"

"She works spells." My hand moved of itself, to straighten my tail.

Amber and I sat together on my couch, trying not to gaze at the Big Womans on my wall. Amber poked her chopsticks into the modest stir-fry we'd concocted. "Perhaps the couch should face the other way."

"It was worse knowing she was in back of me." I clicked my chopsticks toward the wall. "It's better to face straight into it. Reduces the shock of the thing."

"I've been in New York fifteen years, Howard." Amber raised her wine glass, looked into it and drank. "Fifteen long years."

"Perhaps Uqal Mussa could drive us away somewhere for the weekend."

"Who is Uqal Mussa?"

"The Egyptian. Dark fellow, talks about flogging Hyacinth?"

Here she was at last, in my apartment. Surely she could see that apart from the thirty-foot-long, frenzied, drunken Aztec goddess on my wall, my life was that of a sophisticated urban male.

But she seemed to be gazing through me, at the summer night beyond my window. Her sandals were off, Persian creations with busy abstract designs on the inner sole, like pages from the Rubaiyat; she tucked her legs up under her, smoothed her skirt around her knees, and turned her head sideways to The Wall, which gave me the pleasure of her neatly sculpted profile, of aquiline nose and softly squared chin.

"How lovely you are in this moonlight."

"What moonlight?"

"Just a fish tank in the dark, I thought it was moonlight." I moved closer to her, put my arm along the back of the sofa behind her. "We've known each other such a long time."

"Yes, haven't we." She slipped a hand into the pocket of her skirt and leaned back along the couch, her shoulder just a hairsbreadth from my fingertips.

"Intriguing perfume you're wearing." Fingertips creeping down. Contact. The lithe shoulder of a beauty editor.

She turned her face toward me. "Howard, it can never work between us." She removed her hand from her skirt pocket and brought it slowly up to my cheek. "But I suppose that's no reason not to try."

Our arms came around each other, our lips met. I'd thought of this moment so often as I'd gazed from my cubicle to hers, never dreaming the partition between us could fall, that her lips might open to mine as they now did, with the soft surrender of reserve, her passion rising up from hidden depths and promising to shake me to the marrow.

"HALLO, KIDS . . ."

A voice, calling through the air shaft. We turned. In the hallway window of the building across from mine stood Fernando, thumb in the air, sighting toward his Big Womans. *"She look great from here."* Someone stepped in beside him, masked by the shadows of the hall. Then, as Fernando lit a cigar I saw —

"Mitzi Mouse!" I jumped up, called to Fernando. "Why did you take her from the office?"

"I need my model."

I sank back down onto the couch. Amber straightened her skirt, slipped her feet into her sandals.

"Amber, darling, please . . ."

"I said it couldn't work. And this is one of the reasons why."

I stood with her. "Don't go."

She'd reassembled the iron fortress. "Supper was lovely."

"For a moment back there we became two quite different people."

"And now one of us has recovered her senses. Anyone who gets involved with you is crazy." She tightened the straps of her sandals. My hand met hers on her ankle. "Amber, let me do that. You think people will be charging in and out of here all the time? Is that the problem?" I was caressing her adorable calf. "At least stay for dessert."

Her eyes met mine and I wondered: If long ago I'd somehow managed to control my eccentric nature, might I have become that classic Modern Male she sought? No, we become what the IRT subway makes us.

There was a sudden hammering on the door. "Excuse me for just one second, Amber." I opened the door for Fernando and Mitzi.

"Hallo, kid, how you was?"

"I hope we're not intruding," said Mitzi.

Fernando headed toward his wall, stopped beneath it, inserted two fingers in the air, measuring. "Perfect proportion." He was beneath the Big Womans's gigantic hams. He put his fingers to his lips and blew her a kiss. "You beautiful, baby." Then he opened his stepladder and climbed up it, as Mitzi began removing her white deck pants and striped fisherman's shirt.

"I'm going home," said Amber. I opened the door, and we stepped into the hall. The muzzle of a pistol came lightly against my temple; two gentlemen in silk suits were flanking us. "We're taking Mitzi Mouse. Nuncio, go on in."

Nuncio entered my apartment. The sound of a brief scuffle reached us, and then all was quiet. A moment later, Mitzi Mouse was shoved into the hall, completely naked.

"Goddamnit, Nuncio, we can't take her bareass. Go in and grab her coat."

"I din't see one."

"Well, grab somethin', you dumb fuck."

Nuncio went in, and returned with my mail order Italian army officer's trench coat. It fell around Mitzi's bare shoulders.

Amber was nuzzling against me for protection, doing something odd with her hand, what was it? Suddenly the pistol bow came out of her shoulder bag. She spun around, fired, and the arrow skimmed the top of Nuncio's head, taking his fedora with it down the hallway; with a soft thud, the hat was pinned securely to a door. I tried to bolt, and was punched in the face, so hard I went careening backward down the hall, and collided against the arrowed door. It opened behind me and I fell into the arms of my elderly Russian neighbor, Igor Nishtick.

"Michael Most Mighty! Ijim and Dimon-gad! Destroy their figured stones!" Igor took dictation from the angels regarding Jehovah's plans for retribution against mankind, and now, seeing an arrow embedded in his door, he felt the moment had come. I pushed him back inside, slammed the door shut, and threw the long iron police bolt into place.

"We must let the Archangel in!" Igor, reaching for the lock.

I jumped in front of the door. "It's not Michael, it's a pair of gangsters."

"The river Jabbok! The children of Ammon!" Igor shuffled back and forth, waving his fists in the air. I put my eye to the peephole and saw the two hoodlums dragging Mitzi and Amber toward the stairs.

"Howard!" shrieked Amber. "Help us!"

It would do no good for me to rush out and sacrifice myself. More prudent action was needed now. I'd sell my apartment and move to Tenafly.

"Howard! You coward!"

And down she went, Mitzi beside her, both of them held fast by their abductors.

"Og the king of Bashan came against us . . ." Igor had his notebook out now, and dictation had resumed, the old man pacing back and forth, scribbling. ". . . but their livers will be eaten, and their tongues, those of mine enemies . . ."

I went to his window and carefully parted the blinds. Yes, there was the long black mob car at the curb. The back doors opened and Mitzi and Amber were shoved inside. And the dark shame of it was that people were probably watching this abduction from their windows without so much as lifting a hand.

". . . and the Lord said unto me, go, eat the heart of your foe, Nishtick, go and be nourished! Geshem the Arabian! Tobiah and Sanballat!"

I kept presence of mind. "Igor, I am prepared to offer you an exclusive contract for your angelic journals. We can take, oh, say ten pages biweekly, for publication in *Prophecy* magazine."

"How much I get?"

"Five cents a word."

"Mizpah and Hashub!" He hurried to his desk, and I went to the door. A moment later I was back in my own apartment. Fernando was lying catatonic on the floor, two fingers in the air.

I took out the greasy business card of the Aswan Limo Service and dialed. A child answered.

"Is your father there, please?"

"Busy. I help you. You like to buy nice camera?"

"Not at the moment, no."

"How about VCR?"

"I'd like to speak to your father. Tell him it's his new employer."

There was a pause, during which the child breathed thoughtfully into the mouthpiece, then gave a shout for her father. The phone changed hands.

"Who's dis?"

"Mussa, it's your editor in chief. You must come to my place at once with your limo."

"You want sesame dip?"

I gave him the address. "I'll expect you here in twenty minutes." I hung up, dialed Nathan, and told him to get out the blowgun. Then I called Crumpacker, who was unpleasant, of course, but I prevailed and he finally agreed to meet us. I gazed down at Fernando, whose fingers were still stuck in the air. I turned toward his Big Womans. She was slouched indifferently in her hammock, balancing her great medicine ball of a stomach. I walked to the sink, filled a pot with water, and poured it on the artist. His eyelids fluttered, his lips moved, and his hand went to the large red lump on the back of his head. "I kill them." He struggled to his feet, and climbed slowly back up his ladder.

I sank onto the couch. Amber's perfume still lingered there; the cushion bore the imprint of her body. Fernando's ladder creaked, his brush slap-slapped on the wall. I went to the refrigerator and applied an ice pack to my swollen cheek. Prehistoric noises from the throat of the building's super came up the air shaft. "Ahhhrrgggh . . . garrrghhhhh . . ."

Was he biting the heads off rats? Calling to his mate? Or merely expressing appreciation for the latest issue of the *Midnight Examiner*?

The buzzer rang. We made for the lobby, where Mussa performed an obsequious little bow, brushed a piece of lint from my suit, and held the front door for us. "All set, gentlemens, we have fine good time." He scurried ahead to the curb and opened his station wagon. I slipped in, and found myself seated beside a heavily made-up child.

"Mussa, who is this little girl?"

"Najaf. She my daughter." Mussa crawled behind the wheel. "Mrs. Mussa out. I no have the baby sitter."

"We have a dangerous night ahead of us. We can't risk this child."

Najaf tugged at my sleeve. "You want to buy VCR?"

"She very good little girl. Have be smart head for business." Mussa started the car and headed up Riverside Drive. Fernando was studying the girl's face. "How you like to pose for me, kid?"

"Mussa, drive to Eighty-sixth, off West End." I leaned forward and spoke to him more softly. "We must take Najaf back home."

"Mother be angry if I leave Najaf alone." Mussa leaned his head confidentially toward me. "Look, she give you very good buy on VCR."

"I don't want a VCR."

"How abouts microcassette recorder?"

It was only a short ride to Crumpacker's, and he was waiting for us on his stoop, fish pole in hand. I got out and held the door for him. He climbed into the station wagon, beside Najaf. "And who is *this*?"

Mussa spoke over his shoulder. "She save you lots money, Fodder, anything you want. Hi-fi, TV, fancy camera." He nodded toward Crumpacker in his rearview mirror, then gave me a conspiratorial whisper. "I know what clergyman like."

"Downtown, Mussa, to the office."

He swung the wheel, and we circled back along Riverside Drive, and then east across West End, not pausing for stop signs. One quickly accustoms oneself to Egyptian traffic tactics, and resents delay.

Najaf hummed a childish tune, and held up her fingers, fanning them before her and intertwining them, fascinated by her cheaply glittering rings. "I have all kind of calculator, video game, ghetto blaster."

"Mussa, where does Najaf get her merchandise?"

"I know peoples."

"It's hot, isn't it."

"You want oscillating fan?"

Broadway was rushing past us, stores, bars, and restaurants outlined in flickering neon, their denizens creeping through the patterns, human forms upon the electric rainbow, searching for friends, for enemies, for love, or revenge, for some advantage, some scrap of happiness, some opiate to turn the night into an oriental lamp.

"I hope I'm not going to be up late," said Crumpacker.

"Here, you play with me," said Najaf, and took an electronic game out of her purse.

"I'm not good at children's games," said Crumpacker. "In fact, I detest them."

"This not children's game," said Najaf. "This for high rollers."

"It looks impossibly complicated to me." Soon she and Crumpacker were beeping together.

"This is an instant headache."

"You lose!" Najaf was giggling wildly, working herself into a state. "Gimme dollar. OK, now we play again."

Mussa spoke to me quietly. "I like for her be exposed to clergyman."

We rolled down Broadway, past the ruins of an entire block that was being demolished. Up in the skeleton of one of the buildings, dangling from the rafters, I saw a length of shimmering garland, the remnant of a long-forgotten office party, perhaps of a publishing company that couldn't pay the printer, whose editor in chief had suffered the delusion it would last forever, and here was the final bit of glitter hanging now amidst twisted rods, heaps of plaster, caving ceilings.

"Why do the rules keep changing?" complained Crumpacker.

"That's how you do," laughed Najaf, hysterically. "That's how is played this game."

■ ■ ■

Nathan was parked in the vacant lot beside the Chameleon building. "Follow me," he said, and led us to Hudson Street, where we parked across from the White Horse Tavern. Nathan and I went up, through an old factory building converted into apartments. The walls were exposed brick, and the staircase was iron, resounding metallically in the wide bare halls. Hip O'Hopp's place was on the second floor, rear. We rang, and his peephole blinked, showing a magnified bloodshot eye. The door opened.

His apartment was small and dingy. Its most distinctive feature was the ceiling — the paint hung down from it in peeling tongues, some half a foot long. It was like a lunar cheese, with curls coming off it everywhere. Hip caught my glance. "Bits of paint fall in my mouth at night while I snore."

"Why doesn't the landlord fix it?"

"He's offered to, but first I'd have to solve the enormously complicated problem of moving everything into the hallway." He pointed to a cracked leather armchair resting amidst yellowing issues of defunct newspapers piled to the ceiling in cockeyed stacks. "I'd never get things back in order again."

Typewriter and desk formed their own corner, framed by

jumbled encyclopedias, dictionaries, and other reference books, all of them dog-eared and covered with ink spills and coffee stains. The largest clump of dust I'd ever seen lifted gently in the air as we walked past it. "A pet," said Hip, and indeed the object seemed to be following him faithfully around the room. "Tony Baloney lives out on Long Island. He moved to the North Shore a few years ago. I had to go there on a story, and we looked up his place. For future reference." He dressed slowly and carefully before a distorted wall mirror. A cigarette dangled from his lip, smoke rising up past his squinting eyes as he slid the knot of his tie closed.

"This place is a real dump," said Nathan.

"Glad you like it."

"Whyn't you throw out some of these papers? They're blockin' the light."

"I like it dark." Hip put on his jacket, studied himself for a moment in the warped mirror, his reflection surrounded by the stacks of old newspapers in the background. He turned to me, pointed to an opened envelope lying on his desk. "I got some bad news today."

"Income tax audit?"

"A thousand times worse. I was rejected by another monastery." He walked to a round iron wall safe left over from the building's factory days; he opened it and removed a bottle of Jack Daniels. With a heavenward gaze, he said, "If only the bastards would accept me, my old age would be assured. I'd have a roof over my head till I die. Three hots and a cot, my own little cell, and Gregorian chants." He filled three glasses, handed them around.

A framed and aging photo of a belly dancer hung lopsidedly on the wall beside him, signed *With love to Hip*. There were other photos, one of Hip himself in army uniform, looking brash and young and gazing into the future, which was this room.

"The vocation master was a sharp guy. Trained to spot freeloaders. He told me I didn't understand Catholicism, didn't comprehend the monastic movement, wasn't a very loving person, and was deeply disturbed."

"There must be at least one monastery looking for a desperate character like you."

"I've been rejected by all of them. This last one was the bottom of the barrel. They don't make wine and jelly, they don't make nice cookies, they grow scraggly Christmas trees alongside a back highway in New Jersey. Even so, it would've been a solid career move. But it wasn't meant to be." He drained his glass of Jack Daniels. "It's a serious blow to my faith. I sang psalms five times a day, I pruned Christmas trees till my arms ached, I ate their humble porridge, and this cocksucker tells me I'm not a loving person."

He closed up his apartment and we walked downstairs. "I remember when Tony Baloney took over from daddy. Big Joe Baloney had just died in Vegas — some showgirl fucked the old guy to death — and Tony was running the garment center here. Then suddenly he had the whole thing — construction, casinos, Kennedy and LaGuardia airports. He paid off a few debts, killed some friends. He gets indicted, and witnesses vanish."

"We'll get him," said Nathan.

Hip smiled dolefully, crumpled up the monastery letter and threw it in the gutter. "People who screw around with Tony Baloney don't have to worry about old age."

■ ■ ■

Celia Lyndhurst lived close by on Bleecker Street, across from a playground, where we parked. Stepping out I noticed a sign near the sandbox.

CAUTION RAT POISON
HAS BEEN PLACED IN THIS AREA

A nice touch for the children from our ever thoughtful Department of Parks and Recreation. Nathan and I entered Celia's building and mounted the narrow staircase. Nathan had apparently not briefed her properly, for when she opened the door she was wearing a bathrobe and her hair was in a towel. "You'll just have to wait while I dry my hair." As this was three feet long, we had opportunity to spare. "Come on, Howard, you can help me." I followed her through the tiny living room–kitchen into her tinier bedroom. It was impeccably neat, staggeringly so to one of my nature. An ironing board was out, and a pile of newly washed laundry. "I love to iron, don't you?"

"A day without a little ironing and I'd perish."

"Hold my hair sort of spread out in your hands, it'll dry faster that way." We sat on her bed, and her hair dryer started to whir.

Holding Celia's hair, I tried to formulate some plan of action for the adventure ahead, but I'm not good at plans. Celia was the Real Detective, and I'd rely on her, if we ever got her out of her apartment.

"Why did they take Amber?" she asked.

"She fired an arrow at them."

"She's been very moody lately."

"She'd just had supper with me."

"What a shame she was kidnapped."

"Yes, it reinforced certain negative feelings she has about eating with me."

"You couldn't help it." She put her hand to my swollen cheek. "This looks nasty. You must have put up a great struggle."

"I fought valiantly."

She walked to a wall which was covered from end to end by an embroidered gold curtain. Parting it in the middle she revealed her closet, which it would be impossible for one of my limited understanding to describe.

"There are times, Howard, when I can't get out of here in the morning because I don't know who I am. I mean, what is my personal style really supposed to be?" She looked at me, her head moving in its little questioning arcs, those tiny Kali dancer moves. "And do you know what? It's kind of wonderful not to know. I'd better take a sweater in case it gets coolish."

"Take it all," said Nathan from the other room. "We got a station wagon outside."

We followed Celia into the kitchen, toward the door of the apartment. She stopped suddenly, at the sink. "Oh god, I forgot the dishes. I was doing them when you came."

"Hey," said Nathan, "we ain't got time."

"I couldn't possibly leave them."

"Is the Board of Health comin'?"

"Nathan, I'm not like *you*."

"A coupla dishes, a few pans, what's the big deal?"

"It's a very big deal to me, I can't stand coming back to a messy apartment."

"We've got people waitin'."

"I don't want to get *roaches*."

"Everybody's got roaches."

I intervened. "Celia, I have a very simple solution. Would you allow me?" I picked up her pots, pans, dishes, glasses, and silverware and carried them into her bathroom.

"Howard, what do you think you're doing! Why are you putting my dishes in the tub?"

"Trust me. Now we sprinkle in a little detergent . . . like so . . . and now we turn on the shower." The water cascaded down, the detergent foamed up.

"Howard, there'll be *grease in the tub!*"

"I'm adding more grease-cutting detergent, as you can see."

The soapsuds billowed into a huge ball, steam enveloped us, and the dishes disappeared. "Now we just leave the shower running, and when you return your dishes will be done."

"Hundreds of gallons of water will be wasted!"

"Water volume is crucial to this method. Let us close the shower curtain, and now, Celia, let us go."

I gently guided her back through the kitchen, and we descended the stairs, into the street. Celia went ahead with Nathan and Hip in Nathan's car, and our caravan proceeded along Greenwich Avenue, and then on to Eighth Street, behind the crosstown bus heading east, past Giorgio Brutini Men's Shoes, the Eighth Street Playhouse, Samara's Kitchen. Music blared from doorways, and the crowd wound along like a serpent that fragments and joins itself, pieces scattering and recombining at each corner. Two leather-clad youths, possibly readers of *Macho Man,* slouched against a glistening motorcycle and drank beer; their exotic companion, a young woman in leather miniskirt, straddled the seat beside them, her hair styled in spikes, and a tattoo on her leg — a peacock whose long purple and green-gold feathers swept from the girl's thigh to her ankle.

Najaf stared wide-eyed at the resplendent bird. "I want one like that."

"I'll have nothing to do with tattooing a child," said Crumpacker.

"Something small, Crumpacker?" I suggested. "I can't see the harm in it, it'd make a very colorful pictorial."

"She have titties," said Najaf, which effectively silenced both of us. Najaf tugged at Crumpacker's sleeve. "You work at newspaper? Then you know how to make titties grow, yes?"

"No, I do not."

"But I see all the time in newspaper, ladies you want bigger bust."

"They just give you some stupid clamshells to squeeze," said Crumpacker.

Najaf considered this carefully, as our caravan left the lighted facades of the Village behind, and wandered east to the Bowery, and then downtown, through the corridor of raving winos brandishing crutches and bottles, shadows at the bottom of the world.

We turned left on Delancey, heading toward the river: Schwartzbaum Fine English Fabrics, Lichtenstein Tailor Supplies, Golub's Surgical and Trusses. As we passed Orchard Street I caught a glimpse of Shlomo's Fine Designer Fashions, and knew Siggy's domicile must be near. Nathan swerved toward the curb and we pulled in behind him. I stepped onto the sidewalk in front of an optician offering cut-rate contact lenses; a large illuminated eyeball stared at us, then blinked slowly, the lid lowering mechanically down and up. We entered a doorway beside the shop, and climbed a shabby flight of stairs; the Blomberg family lived at the top. Siggy's father opened the door — a small man in sleeveless undershirt and white work trousers. He smelled faintly of vanilla and sugar and his hair was powdered with white flour; the hairs on his forearms were also tipped with white. "Come in, Siggy's expecting. Sig!"

We followed the elder Blomberg down a long, poorly lit hall into the kitchen. Its ancient wallpaper had faded to a pale yellow in which indistinct flowers floated, as if drowned in a flood that allowed only a petal or two to break the surface. Mrs. Blomberg stood at the stove, boiling a bird, the drumsticks of which turned slowly as she stirred. "You'll eat," she said, and put out plates.

"We ain't got time," said Nathan.

Siggy entered the kitchen. "Eat," said Mrs. Blomberg, laying a plate in front of her son. I gazed out the window. A patch of light on the sidewalk directly below grew brighter, then dimmer, then brighter; the eyeball, winking.

"Who we takin' with us?" asked Siggy.

"Everybody," said Nathan.

"The only one who'd be any use is Madame Veronique, but she won't go."

"Sig," said Mrs. Blomberg, "you ask her nice, she'll go."

"Mom, you don't know who we're talkin' about."

"She's home alone?"

"Yeah, probably."

"So she'll go, what else has she got to do?"

"Let's get this show on the road," said Nathan.

"You're in the house of a man who's baked all his life and you don't take a slice of his poppy seed cake?"

"Mom, there's a young woman in trouble —"

Mrs. Blomberg pointed the cake knife at her son. "If you got a girl in trouble, Sig, stand by her." She laid a thick wedge of cake before me. "You eat that while I talk to this son of mine. What's her name?"

"Mouse."

"Probably was Mousekowitz. How many times I remember my zayde telling about those nice Mousekowitzes from Odessa. Siggy, I'm so happy for you."

"This cake is delicious beyond anything I've ever tasted, Mr. Blomberg."

He looked at me, smiled. "Have some more."

"This is plenty."

"You don't like it?"

Sig wrapped half the cake in a napkin, and kissed his mother goodbye.

"Mister, how 'bout you?" She handed me the other half, then fussed with my coat, straightening the pockets. "I like your suit. You shop at Shlomo's too?"

Should there have been any lingering doubt in my mind about my wardrobe, it was gone now, I'd burn it in its entirety.

We went down the stairs, with Mrs. Blomberg calling goodbye from the railing. As we drove away, she waved from her window, and the great blinking eye below stared out at the street, Eye of Horus, Eye of Shiva, Eye of Sheldon Kugelmann, Registered Optician, Over 2000 Fashion Frames in Stock.

"I have a piece of cake for you, Najaf," I said, reaching into my pocket.

"What about me?" said Crumpacker. "I've been sitting out here for hours."

"You're in luck, I seem to have more in this pocket than I thought. Yes, here's half a salami and an apple, let's see what's in the other pocket . . . pair of potato knishes, cream cheese and lox on a bagel, some herring with onion, and a container of noodle pudding."

I spread the feast before us. Mussa opened a thermos of thick, horrible coffee, and as we drove uptown he and Najaf entertained us with a remarkable song about grave robbing, one passed down for centuries in their family and whose lyrics described the best way of entering a tomb without having it collapse on one's head. "It make me homesick," said Mussa. "Alexandria is be such a clean city. You can't see any kind of liquor in the street." He turned to Crumpacker. "Don't worry, they have stores for to sell it to Christians, Fodder."

Yvonne's apartment was on Sixtieth off Lexington. The lobby was small, but its dimensions were complicated by mirrored walls with webs of gold spun through them, in which Nathan and I tried to orient ourselves. A black-tiled fountain played in the center of the lobby, its waters surrounded by potted plants. At its edge was an arrangement of antique chairs and coffee table, the legs of each piece discreetly chained to the floor. The nightman, uniformed in khaki fatigues, looked up at us through a somnolent haze, and adjusted his position. "You kin turn any which way you want in these little chairs but you can't get comfo'ble."

We rode to Yvonne's floor, into a hall troubled by more

gold mirroring, and another antique chair, also chained. Electric candelabra showed the way down the thickly carpeted corridor. "Yvonne's done all right for herself," said Nathan. "I wonder why she's still workin' for me."

"She loves gossip as you and I love life."

We rang Yvonne's bell and she opened the door, wearing a strange garment with gigantic shoulders and a long skirt that proved to be pants when she walked. She looked like the heroine of a science fiction soap opera. Even her wig seemed fuller and wilder, manelike and formidable. Her evening lashes had been attached, and her eyes sparkled with excitement; huge hoop earrings swung at her ears and her wrists were covered with gold bangles. "Darlings, come in, I won't be a minute."

She made her movie queen turn, arm extended as if trailing lengths of chiffon, and left the closing of the door to us. The entrance hall contained a collection of South Sea shells; several of the larger ones were illuminated, and bathed Yvonne in their soft underwater glow, she their Nereid, golden, royal, trailing invisible veils of glory. She led us up the hall and extended her arm again dramatically toward the living room, in which sat baby grand piano, Aubusson carpet, tables in Chinese lacquer, Chippendale sofa and chairs, and four dentists playing cards. "Stanton, you know Nathan and Howard."

"Yeah, sure, make yourself at home, fellas." Stanton Plum cleaned my teeth every six months; at my request he administered laughing gas and charged me extra. He introduced us to his colleagues, who had little interest in anything but the cards in their hands, as Stanton was winning, and the stakes were not low. He tried to confuse them further, telling them about our magazines. "The *Midnight Examiner,* sounds like a paper for dentists who work late, ha ha. And *Young Nurse Romance*, you guys oughta see that, hey Nathan, why don't you start one called *Drilling Young Dental Hygienists?*"

"Stanton, can we just play cards?"

Behind Stanton's head, on a black marble pedestal, was a brightly polished gazelle whose gleaming hooves hovered over their master's bald spot. To his right was a life-sized ceramic baby rhinoceros, its mournful gaze directed into the hand of one of the other dentists, who kept looking at the beast with suspicion. "And then," said Stanton, "we got Howard's tit magazines. Only they got brassieres painted on 'em."

"Yvonne, tell your husband to play cards."

Yvonne was filling her purse — money, keys, derringer, spoon, container of low-fat raspberry yogurt. "Play cards, Stanton."

"I'm playing, I'm playing. You're going out with Nathan and Howard?"

"I'll probably be home quite late."

"So long as I know you're safe."

"There's a possibility we'll be murdered."

"So I'll read about it in *Real Detective*."

I removed my elbow from the snout of the porcelain armadillo I'd been leaning against; its scapular shield of bony plates made me wish that I'd purchased a bulletproof vest for the evening, *Macho Man* advertised one in a lightweight Kevlar. Instead, I'd just have to place my faith in Lady Rana's lucky copper medallion and the camouflage color it had provided me with by turning my entire chest and neck green; I would blend beautifully from the waist up with Tony Baloney's jade plant should he happen to own one, or a pile of oxidizing metal in the junkyard to which my trash-compacted body might be sent.

We followed Yvonne back down the sea-lamped hall, past the glowing shells; where once the vital being dwelled, now a bulb. Remember this, they seemed to say, as you go paddling off.

"They'll sit there all night like four molars," said Yvonne, sweeping into the elevator. She was wearing Giorgio of Beverly Hills, and lots of it; a fragrant cloud would precede us into the Baloney estate.

Yvonne came with me in Mussa's limo, and we followed Nathan's car up Third Avenue. Najaf now sat next to Yvonne. "I'm wishing I had such big clothes," she said, touching the sleeve of Yvonne's science fiction jacket.

Mussa turned back toward Najaf. "You be good girl and maybe Fodder take you shopping."

Yvonne looked at Crumpacker. "What's going on here?"

Najaf pointed a heavily ringed finger at Crumpacker. "Fodder is buying VCR from me."

"Well, it *happens* to be a very good buy." Crumpacker, holding his ground.

"We'll be taking photos of Najaf," I said to Yvonne, "if you want anything for *Teen Idol*. A tattoo may be included."

"Let me see your profile, dear."

"I have cute little nose, yes?"

"I tell you the truth," said Mussa, "Cairo is much more crazy city than New York. Especially to drive, because there all the streets they don't have the white lines to divide so you can take your lane and you know where you go." He said this as he cut diagonally across the avenue to the accompaniment of astounded, squealing brakes behind us. "No, the traffic I don't like it there. Now here we have good signs for the traffic, and the law she help a lot. And I tell you something else, if you have license of the New York, to drive a license, you can get international driver license and you can drive all over the world."

"I'm sure your appearance is eagerly awaited in cities everywhere, Mussa."

"I tell you something. Only part I don't like about New York is the crime. You know sometimes what I say? I wish that one of our rulers comes to run New York for three years. He cut off hands, things change fast, you see."

Mussa swung left, heading west, hand jammed on horn, as traffic halted us. "Mussa, blowing your horn is an act of useless aggression."

"No, is good for you. I always blow when I see —" He pointed toward a sign: FINE FOR BLOWING HORN. "You blow horn, you feel fine, help relieve tension."

Traffic eased, and we shot through behind Nathan, across Fifth Avenue and into Central Park at Ninety-seventh Street. High stone walls ran alongside us, and above them the dark overhang of branches; nature in Manhattan means human nature, except here in Central Park, where tortured grass prevails along with a few thousand trees, in whose gray and dusty arbors hide lovers, Audubon members, and delinquent gangs. Along the fractured concrete paths countless millions of New Yorkers tramp, decade in and out, extracting the essence from their oasis. I myself wander there on weekends, perception distorted by drink, drugs, or jogger's endorphins, depending on which discipline or lack of it I happen to be following at the moment. In the very center of the park there are pockets where one may meditate in relative safety on the life of the park squirrel who knows only these grimy woods surrounded by enormities of sound, gigantic shudderings and bangings of which it can have only the dimmest comprehension. It eats leftover bits of pastrami, french fries, and whatever else appears, a kind of flowering in its meadows, continuous but unpredictable as to location. One hops along and hopes for the best.

We shot out of the park, across Central Park West, and south on Columbus Avenue, past one chic restaurant after another contending for the new gentry's money; we passed the American Indian restaurant where the upwardly mobile West-Sider can eat a buffalo burger, then came Cooper's Cafe, with tables on the street, filled with young professionals. "Not for us," said Siggy, "it's got tablecloths."

And now a parking place. Nathan and I walked around the corner to Hattie's building, whose foyer was graced by a particularly violent piece of graffiti, its letters swollen and primal, a cozy greeting for Hattie after a hard day. The lock on the inside door was broken; we entered the hallway; a single bare bulb illuminated a cracked marble floor covered with cigarette butts and other trash. The hall mirror was split down the center. "The landlord is warehousing the place," said Nathan.

The walls had a hollow ring, many of the apartments already deserted by demoralized tenants. When they'd all been driven out, the landlord would turn the building into a multimillion-dollar condo. We gazed around at the deliberate ruin of a once lovely dwelling. "I tell you, Howard, when I see a thing like this —" Nathan gripped the railing and climbed thoughtfully upward. "— I realize the opportunities for me in real estate."

Hattie's floor had a madman crouched at the end of it for the night, a tattered blanket tucked around him. His head was wrapped in a turbanlike arrangement of hand towels and he was making little warbling noises; if one closed one's eyes one might easily imagine a cageful of budgies at the end of the hall.

I knocked at Hattie's door.

There were scuffling flat-footed steps and a soft click at the peephole. A series of bolts were then thrown, followed by the slow clanking of the sliding police shaft in the floor. Hattie opened the door and peered down the corridor at the huddling looney.

"You know him?" I asked.

"When he crows at four in the morning it can be a pain in the ass."

"How many people are left in the building?" asked Nathan.

"On this floor, just me and the rooster."

"How come you don't move?"

"I'm tough."

When the landlord finally drove her out, Hattie's apartment would be worth two fortunes in today's market; we walked down a long hallway which had a large bedroom on either side of it. These had belonged to her teenage daughters, away at Sarah Lawrence, courtesy of the readers of *Young Nurse Romance*.

We entered a huge living room. The furniture was a mismatched jumble bearing the signs of long abuse by children and complete indifference from Hattie. There were canvas butterfly chairs from the fifties, a few old pieces of what was once Danish modern, a sagging Castro convertible couch piled with books, a coffee table covered with cigarette burns

left by her ex long ago. The only piece that seemed related
to the real Hattie, the inner Hattie, was a shabbily glamorous
floor lamp bearing a shade of dangling colored beads which
called to mind Blanche DuBois, with quite a few of her beads
missing.

Beyond the living room was another, larger bedroom, and
a big kitchen — when the building went condo the insider's
price for this space would be half a million. Hattie had it for
$350 a month. "But the landlord always wins. You saw the
broken door downstairs. Next he'll be hiring junkies to rob
me."

"He won't have to hire them, dear."

"I'll go down with the rooster."

While Hattie went to the bedroom to get herself ready,
Nathan prowled, peering into the other rooms. "Twenty years
ago, Howard, I had a dream. I started a magazine. A small
black-and-white tit monthly. I should have bought a brownstone instead. We're lookin' at four, possibly five studio
apartments here." He slapped his fist repeatedly into his
pudgy palm as he paced the cluttered living room. Hattie
cared little for housecleaning; a rich life of fantasy allowed
her to flop down anywhere and dream, and perhaps she
dreamed more deeply in a cocoon of pillows, papers, stacked
plates, nylons, and empty candy boxes; in a second she could
be on her lover's estate, crushed in his embrace, everything
else behind her, it's just you and me here at Uxbridge House,
he said masterfully, I've given the maids the day off.

I peeked into her bedroom. She had dressed herself in a
Banana Republic T-shirt covered with brightly painted ma-
caws, and a pair of olive shorts from L. L. Bean which left
her skinny knees free to maneuver. She looked more fragile

than ever, as if a firm handshake would destroy her. "Will I need to take money?"

"Nathan is covering all expenses."

"In that case, I'd better take some." She inserted a wallet into her back pocket. Her outfit was completed by a cap with large bill. "Do I look like Beryl Markham?"

"The resemblance is uncanny." I sat on the edge of her unmade bed, and felt it shift beneath me, its warm liquid giving a loud gurgle.

"That's to be my final act in this apartment," she said. "The day I go, I pull the plug."

"After you, *le déluge*."

She slipped her *Macho Man* throwing star into a side pocket, and I flopped back on her bed, a deep feeling of exhaustion coming over me, the result of all the food Siggy's mother had fed us. It was hard to conceive that a full night's adventure, requiring physical exertion, still lay ahead. I dug out a few more caffeine tablets.

"You're going to kill yourself with those things."

"A man riddled with vices."

"Why doesn't some woman take you in hand?"

"You, Hattie?"

"You could do worse."

Why didn't I marry Hattie? She and I had been through so much together, and I knew her resilience, she was pluckier than any of her pale heroines. We gazed at each other now, knowing that we'd each bring the other more comfort and companionship than we were likely to find anywhere else. "It's not meant to be, Hattie dear, as we both well know."

"Amber's a very fine person."

"If cold, vain, and difficult."

"I know her better than you do, Howard. Underneath that chic exterior —"

"There's a heart of quick-drying lacquer." I staggered toward the living room, temples pounding, and a whistling sound in my ears; at such a peak of readiness, I was impatient of further delay. "Everyone ready? Nathan, put away your tape measure."

"You could do like six single-room occupancies if you put another hallway in and took out the kitchen."

"Let them cook on the windowsill," said Hattie.

"Plumbing's the big expense, everybody's gotta have a toilet."

"We can just squat in the backyard." Hattie led us into the hallway. The lunatic was smoking a cigarette now and clucking softly. I noticed that the skylight above him had recently been shattered by a brick, pieces of it and the glass still scattered around in the hall. A shocking incident like this can seriously interrupt regular laying patterns.

We descended the stairs and exited through the broken door. The graffiti painting curved and crept in such a way that it seemed the letters themselves had broken the latch on the door and were about to enter. "The landlord commissioned it," said Hattie. "He'll get his."

We walked back to Columbus. Our staff was out of the cars now, leaning against them and chatting in the soft night air. Were they up to an assault on the armed camp of a Mafia don? Celia pointed at the sky; along with scuba diving lessons she'd also been studying astronomy at the planetarium. "You can always locate the North Star. You just face north and you know, in New York City, it's forty-one degrees."

"I can't see a thing," said Siggy.

"No, the stars are rarely visible, but if you *could* see them, that's where the North Star would be."

Now we were completely oriented. I signaled everyone to get back in their cars, and we headed toward Broadway. "Uptown, Mussa, to Madame Veronique's."

"We go to Atlantic Avenue in Brooklyn for the best falafel of New York."

"Mussa, you almost hit that truck marked Loaded With Explosives!"

"Falafel you have to know how to prepare it. Then you eat and you feel pleasure. It make you strong but not fat. I am a skinny, nobody believe I weigh one hundred eighty-five pound."

Hundred-Eighty-Five-Pound Man Defies Experts, Guess My Weight Says Society Chauffeur.

"And serve with the yoogurt. This is the pleasure. Everything in the life should be pleasure."

We passed Loews theater at Eighty-fourth, then came to a huge square of newly cleared ground framed by green construction fences. I peered out the window at it. "Crumpacker, we both live in this neighborhood. There was once a building there. Now it's gone and *I can't remember what it was*. The city is disappearing before our eyes without a trace. We'll wake up one morning in an alien landscape."

Siggy, mournfully: "We'll wake up at Tony Baloney's with lead weights in our kishkas."

We were stopped at a traffic light. Two young gang members crossed slowly in front of us as the light was changing. Mussa, impatient to be out of the starting gate, blew the horn, then rolled down his window. "Move it, I run you down!" He shot past them as they leapt onto the island in the middle of Broadway. "Law here is very soft," he explained. "In Cairo much more better. Sometimes you say is simple, in this city we have all kinds of people from all over the world and we have different education systems so it's very hard to put all the people in one size."

At the core of this riddle was hidden perhaps the secret of Mussa's self-conviction, but I could not fathom it, no, not I.

"I was nuts about a girl worked on this block," said Sig, nodding toward Ninety-sixth. "I met her one day when I was up this way tryin' to collect some dough from the Lucky Duster."

"That's the yuppie cleaning lady service, isn't it?"

Sig turned around in the front seat to face us with a wounded expression. "You never look at the friggin' ads in our paper, that's your problem. The Lucky Duster sells a little bag of dried cockroach shit or some friggin' thing and you sprinkle it over yourself before you go to a card game or Bingo or the track and it brings you luck."

"And you're the living proof of it, Sig."

"One time I was coolin' my heels in his office and I accidentally broke a bag of that stuff all over myself. It was a hot day, I had my shirt open —"

"You dusted yourself."

"And like an hour later, right down the block on Broadway, at the Argos restaurant, I met Inez."

Yvonne leaned forward; she was a connoisseur of Siggy's love stories, for he had a flair for hopeless situations. "Don't spare the gory details."

"She strung me along for months. I ran errands for her from Westchester to Sandy Hook. I thought she might be capable of the most incredible lewd sex, don't ask me why, because she gave no outward indication that this was true, but somehow I had the notion that if we ever got alone it would be the animals' act."

"And when you got alone?"

"Who got alone? I spent the whole night dipping her pet hermit crabs. If they don't get dipped every half hour their shells fall off."

"I guess that was your animals' act," said Yvonne.

Mussa scooted the car into the curb. We'd arrived at Madame Veronique's. Siggy, Crumpacker, and I crawled out of the car, into the night of upper Broadway. A drug dealer passed next to Crumpacker. "A little toddy for the body?"

"No, thank you."

"The smokin' will get you chokin', but the high will make you fly." He continued on in a smooth liquid glide. An elderly gentleman was coming from the other direction with a scuffling step, several loose pages of newspaper caught on his foot; ignoring their persistent attachment to his person, he just scuffled by; the headline wrapped around his foot was one I'd written myself, about a man in Appalachia who had a tree growing out of his head. Sig saw it too. "Excuse me, sir, I'm conducting a national survey. What did you think of the ad for the easily swallowed miracle weight-loss belly balloon on page twenty-six of the publication attached at this very moment to your right sneaker?"

The Broadway elder shuffled on in silence, and I watched to see when the *Midnight Examiner* would work loose from his shoe and fall to the gutter, but the sheer force of editorial substance kept it attached. We entered Madame Veronique's hall. The same old woman we saw last time was coming down the stairs.

"Good evening," I said.

"I ain't seen nuttin'."

"You haven't seen *anything*," said Agnes T. Wimple.

"Good, 'cause I ain't seen it." She hobbled out into the street. We turned and climbed up the stairs.

"If Madame V don't go with us, we're gonna get froshed," said Siggy, lugubriously leading the way, one hand on the railing, the other pulling at the seat of his pants. Madame V herself opened the door, without our knocking. "I don't suppose you brought any pizza." She wore a red taffeta dress, layered in swirls at the bust and opening into ruffles that fell to below the knees. A red turban swathed her head, held fast by a silver clasp.

The outer office was dim, lit only by a votive candle; the sealed boxes of her mail order business were stacked and ready for tomorrow's post. There was no sign of the three goombahs we'd left there earlier. The air was heavy with the scent of incense and steeping tinctures through which Madame Veronique led us into her sitting room, where I explained the situation to her.

She removed her shoes with a groan and elevated her feet on an embroidered hassock. "I see . . . yes . . . much mischief has been done." She turned to Crumpacker. "And you, slim-jim, how are you this night?"

"I just lost half my week's salary playing beep squares with an infant."

"It's the heat, it's got me in a mess too, and I got a big hoodoo meeting to go to. And look at the color of these stockings of mine supposed to be sheer support. That look like sheer to you?"

"We were hopin' you'd come with us," said Siggy.

"I got other doings on tap."

"These guys'll screw us to the wall, Madame V."

"I've got to whip up a gatherin' and I'm feeling big as a house." She shifted uncomfortably as she tugged at the midsection of her dress. "There's going to be a gentleman there, a Haitian diplomat who used to be crazy about me. We've not seen each other for years and all day I been worrying about the way I look. So you know what I did? I ate steady from the time I woke up this morning until five minutes ago when you arrived."

"You've gotta help us," said Siggy.

"Magazine man, I cannot help myself, that is the problem for tonight. When he saw me last I weighed a hundred pounds less. I was the flower of the island." Madame Veronique heaved herself up, shoved her feet in a pair of floppy slippers, and shuffled over to one of her shelves. "Well, I was told he's not in such hot shape himself any longer, but his eyes will still be looking at me." She took a bottle off the shelf and held it at arm's length, trying to read the label. "I cannot see this, where are my glasses?" She looked toward us, and we immediately began a search around the room, which proved unsuccessful. Madame V stepped over to me, took my glasses off my nose. "Yes," she said, putting them on, "these will do. Now what have I got here, I wonder . . ." She scrutinized the container she held in her hand.

"Looks like a squid in a bottle, Madame V," said Siggy.

"So it is." Madame V gave the bottle a shake, and the dead rubbery arms gestured limply in an eternal sea. "We don't want that. One sip, magazine man, and your walnuts would shrivel."

"Skip that one," said Siggy, gently uncrossing his legs.

She set it down and walked on, her slippers scuffing along the floor. Crumpacker, Siggy, and I watched her in silence as she combined some powders, stirring them with a demitasse spoon. Then she turned to her liquids, taking a bit from this bottle and that, pouring them into a little vial. A warm breeze entered the window, searched the room, and left, taking with it the hundredth part of Madame Veronique's tincture to blend with the potion it was making, the wind's own mixture for the Broadway lizards wandering below. The drug was circulating, through doorways and windows, spun in through fans, circling the sleepers, troubling their dreams.

Madame Veronique stoppered the vial with a cork, and stared down at me over the rims of my own glasses. "Doctor, I contemplate joining an organization of fatties called Take Off Pounds Sensibly."

"Laudatory, Madame V. It might be the answer."

"Would that I had joined it many months ago. I'd not be splitting this dress at the seams tonight." She gave the ruby red vial to me. "Drink this."

"Now?"

"When circumstances decree."

"How will I know?"

"You will know." She handed a white packet to Crumpacker. "You must rub this on your member."

"I have no intention of rubbing anything on my member."

"Then upon your forehead. And this —" Madame Veronique gave Siggy another, larger packet. "— is for you. It will make you a ball of lightning."

"Look, Madame V, all that jazz is fine, but we need you in person."

"Come with me, magazine men. I wish to show you something I would show to no others."

"This'll be hot stuff," said Siggy to me. "The real mumbo jumbo."

We followed her through the candlelight, into her kitchen. She stepped to the refrigerator and pulled open the freezer. "Look," she said. "Look at that."

It was filled with pints of ice cream. Häagen-Dazs.

"Is this not a sinful thing?" she asked.

I put my arm around her shoulder, turned her from the freezer. "I have a drawerful of cookies at home, Madame V. We all do these things."

"When Malabar sees me tonight, he will ask himself what happened to that slender girl."

"She's going to Take Off Pounds Sensibly. Siggy, Crumpacker, confiscate the ice cream."

We left her a small Dixie cup in the back of the freezer, took the rest in a plastic shopping bag. "If there's ice cream around, Madame V, it will be eaten. That is one of life's great truths."

She removed my glasses from her nose, handed them back to me. "I shall go into my meeting as saucy as can be. If Malabar don't like me, he is the loser. All is in the hands of the Djab."

She ushered us back out into the hall and closed the door on us. I had the vial wrapped in my handkerchief and I'd know the time to drink it. Wouldn't I?

The street awaited us, along with our Chameleon staff, and once again our caravan departed. We devoured ice cream, and Najaf got hyper from sugar. "You buy radio and camera from me, Fodder?"

"A VCR is all I can afford," said Crumpacker. "I'm rather extended right now."

"I take ten percent down and you make twenty-dollar-a-month easy payment."

"Little girls shouldn't sell merchandise of questionable antecedents while their mouths are full of pistachio ice cream."

"If you buy radio and camera I throw in nice wristwatch." We were following Nathan across town toward the East River and ran into some traffic outside an all-night grocery store, owing to a murder just committed; the body was lying on the sidewalk with a sheet over it, and police cars were two-deep on the street. A few shoppers came and went, stepping around the corpse with their packages. Mussa gestured toward the scene of the crime. "For what he stick the place up? For five dollar? Ten dollar? Is much more different in Cairo. If you are making shopping over there, and the owner need to go to the bathroom, so he closes a long stick over the door. No more. Just a long stick. I am young man then, I say to him, you are crazy, even you leave this door open with four policemen you can't leave one second, he say no. I learn from that man, because you know why? He tell me something I never forget. In Cairo nobody steal for five dollar. In Cairo when they want to steal is for hundreds of thousands. I never forget. From then on I know how I must do."

We were all, I think, grateful for this display of moral certitude.

"Stop car," said Najaf. "I must be throwing up at once."

Fernando and Crumpacker took Najaf outside and held her while she retched in the gutter. She returned to the car, sniffling good-naturedly. "Eat too much ice cream."

"I'll tell you a story," said Fernando, settling in beside her.

"What about?"

"A cow in a dress."

"Sound good, go ahead, please."

We traveled out of Manhattan, Uqal tailgating Nathan's Jaguar, so close I could see Nathan's concerned expression in his rearview mirror. He kept waving Mussa off, and Mussa waved back, smiling, as he pressed closer, inches from the Jaguar's bumper.

"My first husband drove this way," said Yvonne. "Every breath he drew was a territorial dispute."

". . . and the great big cow was big as a wall."

"How she get so big?"

"Because Fernando paint her that way, now you listen to this next part."

"When does she get pretty dress?"

"Is coming."

We reached the Long Island Expressway in the light traffic of those souls who wander at night, bearing their dream along on wheels to unknown rendezvous, read all about it in the *Midnight Examiner*.

". . . was the most wonderful dress a cow ever had, covered with pink flowers."

"The dress which you pay three hundred dollar for here, you can buy in Cairo one hundred dollar." Mussa, gesturing in the rearview mirror. "This shirt cost me two dollar in Alexandria. And I like it much more better than the shirt we have it here in New York."

Najaf cuddled her head down into Fernando's lap. And soon she was asleep, with Fernando watching over her, his fingers lightly stroking her hair. We all fell silent for a while then, listening to the child's little snores. The dark roadside foliage rolled past us, punctuated by glowing highway lamps, while overhead airliners twinkled as they circled, bringing in executives with attaché cases, lowering them down slowly in order to place them completely in the chaos. We reached the Glen Cove exit in less than an hour, and turned onto a small back road.

Yvonne pointed. "*That's* Piping Rock Country Club. It's so chic they wouldn't let Jackie Onassis in."

"I get you in," said Mussa. "I know how you do."

Only darkness and trees, and the emanations of old money.

"What am I doing out here?" asked Crumpacker. "I'd promised myself tonight I was going to beat my mattress."

"Needs a good thrashing every now and then, does it?"

"Futons *all* sag in the middle. I pound it back into place with a heavy broom handle."

"*Ladies Own Monthly* readers should have this technique, old man."

The road continued on through the densest sort of woods, broken only by occasional twin pillars of stone to which high iron gates were fixed, and beyond them, curving drives caught briefly by our headlights. Nathan's Jaguar had slowed to a crawl now, and at each gate Hip's head turned toward the window. I could feel him peering through the alcoholic mists, his old newspaperman's radar scanning for the familiar blip. Suddenly he was pointing toward a fortresslike wall. Nathan maintained an even speed, and we cruised along beside the wall of the estate for what must have been many acres, before it angled off into the darkness. Nathan drove on until we reached a turnout in the road, belonging to the county, for there was a deserted picnic area there by the edge of a stream. We parked and got out for a conference of war in the cool night air.

"Our strategic objective is ahead of us." Nathan sat on a picnic bench, blowpipe between his legs, and the rest of us gathered around him, but I was listening to the stream beyond us in the dark, its voice suggesting watery solutions from the depths if one could but understand, and then I realized it was Madame Veronique whispering in my mind:

Call upon the Djab . . .

Yes, it was definitely she, I knew that husky voice, honey smooth, imperious. I drifted away from the picnic bench, into the trees. How does one call upon the Djab?

"Unaccustomed as I am . . ." I walked toward the stream, muttering quietly. ". . . we'd take it as a great honor and privilege . . . Djab could be of assistance . . ."

The stream was before me, slipping along with the moon on its back. The smell of pine needles was strong all around me, so strong and suggestive I remembered a lifetime as a rabbit, hopping around in the perfume of nature, covered by it, drunk with it, little Howard Hare. I took out Madame Veronique's vial and held it up. A tiny moon was caught in its glass, meant to be swallowed.

I gulped it down, not without a tremor of fear, but Madame V was a trusted advertiser who'd passed our stringent standards of product testing.

A bitter liquid, at best. Hits the stomach with a thump. Now what?

I looked around me. The world was much the same as it was before. I returned to our group.

They were bickering, of course, in whispers, seated around the table like a pack of raccoons. Najaf was at the end of the bench, swinging her legs back and forth, her flat little shoes skimming the grass with rhinestone glitter. "Mussa, we cannot take Najaf with us."

"She come in handy, you see. Fit in places nobody else get to."

"Absolutely not. She's to stay here with you, out of danger."

He saluted. "Is in the car."

Did this mean yes? I turned to Nathan, who was punching the dark with his stubby fingers and speaking directly from the pages of *Macho Man*. "We're looking at a night operation here. We chop our way through the bush and take the wall by main force."

"Why don't we just wade upstream," said Yvonne. "It would cover the sound of our footsteps."

"No," said Celia, "you can drown in four teaspoons of water."

We'd be standing there yet, except for Fernando, who charged ahead into the leaves, and we followed. I suppose a herd of grazing brindled gnu might have made more noise; everywhere one steps in the woods there is something crackling underfoot, and the huge shoulders of Yvonne's outfit snapped branches on both sides of her as she went forward.

Hip was in front of me, weaving to and fro, letting out yelps of surprise when touched by a leaf or bush. This was quite possibly the first time in his life he'd actually been off a sidewalk. How would he be under fire? Only the Djab knows.

And then a curious thing took place: When I looked where Fernando was leading, I saw him and the trees around him as clearly as in daylight.

"Yvonne, I'm seeing in the dark."

"Howard, I'm sinking in mud." Yvonne had walked into a spiderweb and I could see it shining on her cheeks and forehead, each strand perfectly clear, like threads of crystal, the Djab's work, surely.

And suddenly, I had a telepathic view of the goombah compound, floating in a bubble before my eyes. There was a guard just inside the main gate, sitting on a stone bench, smoking and staring at the ground.

And I could hear his thoughts.

. . . out here in the fuckin' dark every fuckin' night. I feel like a fuckin' owl. What the fuck was that? That a noise in the fuckin' woods?

I threw up my hands to the group. A silvery net seemed to float out of my fingers and land around them, and they all froze in place, looking at me with questioning gazes. I put a finger to my lips.

Just some fuckin' animal. Tear my balls off I go out there.

I kept my hands in the air, holding the group in stillness.

Fuckin' place gives me the creeps. Gimme fuckin' Brooklyn every fuckin' time. You got pizzerias, boccie courts, you know where you are. Here, you got weird fuckin' shit comin' at you from the moment you fuckin' wake up. Hey, what's that . . .

I saw Mussa with his nightstick in the center of my bubble, standing over the now unconscious guard. Najaf was beside him, dancing around excitedly. The bubble popped and I signaled everyone forward quickly, to the wall. I formed my hands into a cup and Siggy took a running start, stepped into my hands, and heaved himself up the wall. His pants ripped at the seat as he went over with a grunt; Shlomo would have to answer for that.

The rest of us followed, dropping to the ground on the other side of the wall. Mussa bound and gagged the goombah, took his pistol, then rolled him in back of the stone bench.

Nathan stepped up to him. "I like that kind of initiative." He turned to me. "Remind me about a decoration for this man."

I scanned the grounds, the white gravel footpaths as clear to me as if they'd been illuminated by spotlights. I crept in beside Crumpacker. "Rub on Madame Veronique's powder, it'll help you to see in the dark."

"I don't believe in it, I don't trust it, I don't approve of it, and what if I become hopelessly addicted?" He opened the packet and tapped its contents into his palm. Then, very cautiously, he applied it to his forehead. "It *feels* like an instant case of hives."

Hattie, Celia, and Yvonne were kneeling beside the unconscious goombah. In an earlier culture they'd have been removing his privates, but Yvonne settled for taking his charge cards.

I heard the sound of a door opening somewhere on the estate. The bubble appeared in front of my eyes again, bringing me a close-up view of the side porch of the main house, off which a sleek Doberman pinscher was leaping, teeth bared. *"Dog!"* I hissed, and everyone heard it, a low growling coming quickly toward us.

"Lemme try an' deflect it," said Siggy, taking a length of

Mrs. Blomberg's salami from his pocket. He moved forward, waving the salami enticingly as the Doberman charged through the trees. "Here, boy," said Siggy, though it was not necessary to summon the beast, as it was streaking directly toward him, snapping its jaws. Siggy knelt, underpants showing in the moonlight through the huge split in his seat. What drove our advertising director to this rash act of heroism? Could it be Crystal Courage as advertised on page thirty-five of this week's *Midnight Examiner,* ten dollars a crystal plus two dollars' postage?

"Salami like this you don't get every day, poochie."

The dog sprang. I heard a soft whistling sound near my ear, and the dog gave a yelp, then turned a clumsy somersault over Siggy, and hit the ground with its legs buckling under it, a dart from Nathan's blowpipe in its side. It kicked a few times, and rolled over, twitching through drugged doggie dreams. Fernando and Hip lifted the sleeping animal carefully, carried it to the wall and dumped it outside the estate.

I moved across the lawn. The trees turned silver, with shafts of unnatural light playing through them, and then the scene became its own negative, and I saw the main house clearly — neo-Georgian, faced in stone. Beside it were garages, stables, toolsheds. All quiet. Ah, but there, on the front porch of the main dwelling, another goombah.

Crumpacker came up beside me, Najaf behind him, clinging to the end of his fishing line so as not to get lost. Contemplating the goombah, I heard low rumblings in my ear, like ball bearings rubbing against each other, and then my auricular muscles twitched, and all was clear:

. . . *shoulda folded on that last hand, alrigh', so I lost a coupla sawbucks . . .*

Then, from the corner of my eye, I saw Najaf skipping on ahead, her tiny shoes glittering. Crumpacker dove after her, but she was on past him, prancing up the path. He looked at me in alarm; I signaled him to remain quiet, and we both crept forward.

Jesus Christ, am I seein' things, it's a little hooker comin' up the path, hey it must be a joke the guys are pullin' on me, where'd they find that little broad?

"Hey, little lady, how you doin' tonight?" The goombah stepped off the front porch, and the cardinal and I closed in, Crumpacker whipping the handle of a garden hoe down on the goombah's head, as if on an irregular futon.

We dragged him into the bushes as Najaf danced around us, her sequined stockings sparkling in the moonlight, and then she was off again, rushing ahead through the dark. I put the goombah's pistol in my pocket, and Crumpacker and I joined the others behind a low hedge that lined the pathway to the house.

A large pond was nearby, moonlight rippling on its surface and a Japanese bridge arching over it. One did not wish to know who might be at the bottom. The air was thick with scent from the flower beds surrounding the pond, and here Tony Baloney probably spent much time writing haikus, and here the entire staff of Chameleon Publications was crouching.

"I love it," said Celia. "I mean, you can see that the person who lives here really cares for every tree and blade of grass."

Clouds passed before the moon, then set it free again; a whippoorwill was calling somewhere in the trees. And now a frog began ga-rumping in the pond, to be joined by another and another. Hip looked toward them suspiciously.

"Frogs, Hip. Little green things that swim?"

He shook his head. Out of his element entirely.

"What are we going to do now, Nathan?" Yvonne was straightening the enormous shoulders of her outfit in preparation for the next plunge through the Magnetic Line.

"It's a tough call. We gotta penetrate the bunker."

"Let's try the decoy trick again," said Hattie. "But I think a maturer figure would be more effective."

"I'm gonna go up that thing." Nathan pointed at a luxurious growth of ivy branching out beneath a bedroom balcony. "Siggy, you cover me from below, and follow in a zigzag fashion, making a low silhouette. The rest of you attack any way you can." Nathan went across the lawn, his roly-poly figure crouching, then flattening out against the base of the chimney. A second later, he was climbing through the leaves.

"We don't want to commit our entire force to the house," I said. "Hip, you and Hattie stay out here. Mussa — where is Mussa?"

"He and the girl go 'round the side," said Fernando. "I go that way too." He followed through the box hedges, and disappeared into a faint bluish maze of columbine. Celia and Yvonne moved off, along the edge of the main path. I looked at my watch. Both hands were pointed at twelve. The *Midnight Examiner* had struck.

Crumpacker and I headed toward the back, crouching along between rows of ginkgo trees. The low canopy of yellow leaves gave way to the green of oaks, their shadowy tops much higher, their big trunks wrapped with a fleshlike bark that made them seem like huge bodyguards, eager to crush us if their limbs could just reach down. "My forehead's puck-

ering," said Crumpacker. "If I *had* rubbed that powder anywhere *else* —" He pivoted around, slowly.

"What is it?"

"Why, I'm seeing . . . an alligator! He's . . . he must
be . . . at *that* window!"

Crumpacker whirled with his pole, casting into the dark,
line spinning out, reel clicking delicately. Yes, he was a mas-
terful fisherman in broad daylight, but could he possibly hope
to hook anything in total darkness? Pray to the Djab.

"Thon of a bith . . ." A figure lurched through the window
and plunged downward, clawing at his lip. He hit the ground
with a thump, and rolled over in pain as Crumpacker quickly
wound in the slack. The speckled goombah is noted for the
fight he puts up once hooked, thrashing wildly and then making a desperate leap toward freedom, but I struck him unconscious with a small stone vase, then gagged him with his
own socks; as he wore no belt with which I could tie him,
I had to ask Crumpacker for his.

"Use your own belt," said the cardinal.

"In case you haven't noticed, I'm wearing the fashionable
new elasticized waistband as found only in the finest polyester
creations."

"Oh, for god's sake, here," said Crumpacker. "It's lizard
and very expensive."

"You'll be reimbursed by our treasurer."

"Who the hell is that?"

"The office has yet to be filled."

We bound the goombah securely and dragged him behind
a shed, not before mercifully removing the plumed hook from
his lip. "You take his pistol, old man, then we'll each be
armed."

"No," said Crumpacker, "I'm liable to shoot myself with it."

I rammed the second pistol into my elasticized waistband. Hattie came hopping along like a sandpiper, her white knees poking up through the darkness into the moonlight; one thought for a moment she might take wing, but then she crashed into the shrubbery. Little flowers scattered as she struggled out of the bushes and crept over to us and our prisoner. "Poor dear, he's just a baby, hardly more than a teenager."

"Yes, I imagine he just got out of the Boy Scouts."

"My Beautiful Lover Is In The Mob. Please, Won't Some Reader Out There Help Us?" She was going through his pockets. "Where do they go wrong?" she asked herself. "Is It All Because Of A Woman?"

"Take this vase, and if he wakes up, crack him on the head."

"Did he ever have a suitable role model?"

"Hattie, can I trust you to keep him tied up? Even if he opens those long lashes and looks at you with whispered love words?"

"How can he whisper, Howard, he's got a sock in his mouth."

"What happened to Hip?"

"I saw him making amorous noises at a frog."

"Whom he hoped would support him in his old age."

"All he's ever known is barrooms and restaurants, Howard. This is an opportunity for him to appreciate the Raw Throbbings Of Nature."

I turned back toward the house. "Crumpacker, come along, we've got to get in there."

He pointed magisterially to the open window through which the speckled goombah had been caught. "Would you please hold my fishing device?"

"An honor, Crumpacker."

He climbed up, and I followed him in through the window. Our prisoner had been seated in a corner of the library beside a wall of leather-bound, gold-tooled books bought by the linear foot. A small shaded lamp shone over the now empty chair. On the table beside it was an unfinished bottle of soda, half a bag of potato chips, and a copy of the latest *Midnight Examiner*.

We inched out of the library into a long carpeted hall, the other end of which was lost in distant darkness. The mansion was enormous, one could feel the solemn space of it now. Tony Baloney would be accustomed to the soft voices of his staff by night, and their footsteps in the corridors. I felt we could proceed.

A chandelier of white porcelain flowers hung overhead. Niches filled with marble statuary lined the hall. We made our way slowly along. The walls were done in fanciful Chinese wallpaper, elephants depicted on it, with royal saddles bearing the entourage of some potentate toward a brightly colored jungle where monkeys swung. The procession was interrupted here and there by doors leading to other rooms, all empty, no sound or light coming from them. The hall itself was lit by small single flame-bulbs; there was a long mahogany table holding nothing but the reflected glow of the lamp positioned above it. In the adjacent niche was a bronze statue of Justice holding a pair of scales. Next, a large vase filled with lilies. And then an antique chair squatting by itself at the end of the hall, at the juncture of another, larger hall, where Uqal Mussa was stuffing his pockets with objets d'art. He saw us and waved. We hurried over to him.

"Mussa, this is not the time for larceny."

He looked at me in confusion. His family had been tomb robbers for centuries, and in the excitement of our breaking and entering, the long-buried profession had understandably surfaced from the ancestral depths. I grabbed him by the sleeve and hurried him into a high-ceilinged drawing room, where Fernando was standing upon a table, charcoal in hand, covering a large white wall with violent strokes.

Mussa pocketed an ivory stork, two gold candlesticks, and a Chinese bowl. The living room was, for my taste, rather a jumble — filled with classical busts, collections of silver boxes, netsuke, Fabergé eggs, but Mussa was speedily transforming it into a simpler composition. Crumpacker had collapsed on a Récamier sofa, frantically scratching his puckered forehead. I entered another large sitting room furnished with armchairs and couches, on one of which Celia sat, hands in the lap of her skirt. "Howard, it's absolutely perfect here. I think it would be very unfair of us to drag Amber away."

"Let's not lose our editorial objectivity. Amber was abducted at gunpoint by bloodthirsty killers."

"Bloodthirsty, rich killers, Howard." Celia drew her legs up under her on the couch. "Amber's a charming woman; she's made an impression, I'm sure."

"We'll be lucky if she hasn't been put in a garbage disposal unit."

"You don't know what a woman can do when she sets her mind to it." Celia leaned back into the deep cushions. "It's *so* comfortable here. I feel like a little oink-oink."

"Oink oink?"

"A greedy, materialistic person, Howard. I spend all my weekends window-shopping on Madison Avenue. If it were I who'd been kidnapped, I'm not sure I'd try to get away, I might make the most of a dynamic situation. I mean look around you — this is Louis furniture, that's a Louis tapestry on the wall, those are Louis dogs on the mantelpiece. I think we should wait for Mr. Baloney to wake up, and then explain our concern for Amber, which will help to place her in the right light for him as a woman with a wide circle of friends and admirers, among whom we have to count you, Howard, and I know this whole affair is hard on you emotionally because of your involvement with her, but I think you have to just step aside and let the polarities evolve. I mean I don't have the wardrobe for a house like this, but Amber does, she's had more years to shop, and she's going to look perfectly at home in these surroundings, and after that who knows, bonding may occur."

Mussa had by now stripped the mantelpiece bare, and was leaving the room with an embroidered pillowcase full of loot. I followed him to the main hall, whose curved staircase opened out ahead of us, left and right, ending in a pair of carved ebony sphinxes. Down these stairs Tony Baloney had come how many times, his modest dream secure, his goombahs watching at every door. He had anxieties, to be sure, but they did not include a team of magazine editors entering in the night with a hereditary tomb robber.

Where were Mitzi Mouse and Amber?

Were they undergoing a humiliating interrogation? Lurid headlines circled in my brain, but I had no time to write them down. Hopefully I would remember them in the morning.

Mussa was unscrewing a gold-plated light switch. I peered up the staircase toward the landing, where a marble nymph demurely covered her breasts.

"We take along," said Mussa.

"Too large, Mussa."

"No problem."

Guided by his ancestors, Mussa lifted the nymph and carried her downstairs. Glancing out the window that graced the landing I saw Siggy staring in at me, a frantic look on his face as he clutched the crumbling vine. His gaze went from keen distrust of the ivy to a special loathing for it entirely as it cracked in half and he slid sideways off the face of the building, into shadow.

Crumpacker and I pressed on, up the curving stairs to the second-floor hall. Here the walls were covered with a fleur-de-lis linen and lined with framed cartoons from *Punch*. Nothing from *Knockers* and *Bottoms*? An oversight surely.

We were in the heart of the enemy stronghold. The walls held the secrets of Tony Baloney deep within their fabric, which Crumpacker seemed to dislike; it was a bit too florid I suppose; *I* liked it, but then my choice of fabric had been called into question so many times that I felt incompetent to judge.

A peculiar twitch came in my auditory nerves; my ears rotated forward like a bat fine-tuning to the sonar bounce, and I heard the voice of Madame V in the darkness:

Long has hoodoo been suppressed. I refer you to Supreme Court of Jamaica's decision in 1867 which made it unlawful to possess the implements of Obeah.

Madame V at her meeting. Addressing fellow practitioners.

From that date, everyone practicing Obeah was to be arrested.

Prophecy magazine stuff. Must talk to Crumpacker about it.

Right were they to fear it, friends. For it belongs to Djab.

Dear old Djab. Been awfully good to us so far. Concentrate, concentrate. Each step is danger now.

I pointed for Crumpacker to open the door directly ahead of us. He turned the knob and pushed gently.

Only a bathroom. Bigger than my entire apartment. Much room is needed to wash Mr. Baloney, get his pores open and singing. Black marble. Gold faucets, Mussa will see to those. Amidst all this splendor, two jarring touches: an extra roll of toilet paper covered with a frilly cozy, and a small ceramic frog with a soap pad in its jaws. Stitched in red and green thread on one of the towels were the words YOU'RE A VERY SPECIAL GUEST. Could it be that somewhere in this castle there dwelt a reader of *Ladies Own Monthly*?

Crumpacker pointed to the other end of the bathroom, to a connecting door. We crossed the vast ablution area, its heavy carpet silencing our steps.

I took the knob in my hand, turned it, and pushed.

The room was large, lit by a torch lamp held in the upraised hand of a small bronze Nubian slave. Yvonne was in the middle of the room, seated on the edge of a canopied bed, derringer in hand. "Howard, Mother has made a tragic discovery. I've spent my life in the wrong profession. I should have been a private investigator." She flung herself back on the bed, sighed, looked at the ceiling. "You get to snoop around in other people's houses."

"It's not too late. Celia advertises a mail order course in

Real Detective. A complete criminology kit is included, with badge, for fourteen ninety-five plus shipping and handling."

"I feel I have the gift for it." Behind her on the bed was a pillow on which was embroidered, WHOEVER HAS THE MOST TOYS WHEN HE DIES WINS. She sat back up, head turning sharply.

"What is it, Yvonne? Do you hear something?"

She sprang off the bed, sniffing at the air. "Somebody *else* is wearing Giorgio." Angrily squaring the outrageous shoulders of her outfit, she stomped toward the door. "I'll get to the bottom of this." And out she stormed.

Crumpacker and I followed, in time to see her disappear into the nether regions of the corridor. We started after her but were immediately forced back into the shadows by the sight of a figure stepping out of the next room — a strange, almost ghostly figure, of a woman in white. She paused, looked around as if sensing she was being watched, but Crumpacker and I were invisible in the darkness, our backs pressed into one of the alcoves.

We watched her then, this mysterious figure, as she slowly paced the hall. She came quite close to us, a tall woman of strong features accented by mauve-shadowed eyes, trapped eyes. She turned and paced the other way, clearly a prisoner in this tower. She moved with lifeless steps, like the medieval unicorn, a white creature of fantasy, penned on every side. Thus would Amber turn out, if she didn't go to the garbage disposal unit first.

Crumpacker and I watched the pitiful creature walk off, scarf trailing sadly behind her. How had she been captured? And why? She paused at the end of the hall, then slid away into the shadows, to whatever room was hers in this gilded cage.

"We must free her as well as the others, old man, you know that don't you?"

"My cats are going to be *so* cranky if I'm not home soon." Crumpacker ambled off in the direction the mystery woman had taken, and I followed, past fifteen framed views of Windsor Castle. He stopped beside a marble-topped commode in the hall, its gilt legs shaped into lion's claws, and a woman's gilt face carved into either side of its gilt-latched drawers. "Yes, it's expensive." He ran his finger along the marble edge. "But tacky is tacky."

"I'm grateful for this lesson in taste, Crumpacker."

"Who does he think he is, the Sun King?" Crumpacker, disdainfully, leading the way. We turned into the next wing, where the white-clad woman had gone. A rock crystal chandelier hung overhead, icily glowing in moonlight streaming in from an adjacent window. We paused at the window and looked down. The pond was visible through the trees, its surface calm. I clutched Crumpacker's sleeve. A figure was moving in the garden. We watched as it crept along beside the house. The figure's hand went to the seat of its pants. Siggy! Yes, definitely, there's the flash of his underwear as he turns . . . and now he disappears like the shy white-tailed deer, into the box hedge.

We drew back from the window. "Crumpacker, what do we do? There must be fifty rooms in this place."

"My cats are peeing in the sink."

"You can't know that for sure, Crumpacker."

"I just *saw* them doing it."

"Direct your voodoo powers toward the situation at hand, old man. What's down this hall?" I pointed him forward, held him steady.

"*All* I can see are those cats acting up."

"Wonderful creatures, Crumpacker, but you've let them become an obsession."

"My cats are what keep me going when all else fails."

"And no one's rebuking you for it, but if you would just concentrate on this hallway."

And then suddenly my own voodoo vision returned. One room after another appeared to me. I seemed to be in a Neapolitan palace, the fifty rooms become a hundred. I felt enormous stone extensions, turrets, battlements, and realized I was in Tony Baloney's dreams, in the alchemy of his desires, where he reigned as noble lord.

 . . . *did I get taken on those eighteenth-century chairs? And what about the Regency four-poster? It don't seem old. I've spent all this dough, and I got no way of knowing because I'm just a thickheaded wop from Brooklyn. Well, fuck 'em, I got those Medici lap dogs, and that Roman amphora, I know it's genuine. Don't I? No, Tony, you got no way of knowing. You're in the hands of your decorators, who knows what kind of shit they're pulling?*

"Crumpacker, I'm in Tony Baloney's dreams. I'm hearing his basic insecurities."

"Where are we?" asked Crumpacker, shaking his head from side to side. "I was just in my apartment."

"We're in Baloney Palace, Crumpacker." We passed an armless Apollo staring out of a shadowy niche. The stony eyes drilled into mine, and I felt a wave of sympathy for Tony Baloney, the Mafia don who wanted to be Old Money.

I got a whole house full of stuff. Some of it's got to be real. No, Tony, none of it has to be real. It could all be crap. They could be turning it out in a cellar in Taiwan, you wouldn't know the difference.

"He's a tortured man, Crumpacker. Everything he owns torments him."

"Yes, and I can see why." Crumpacker pointed toward a pair of Olympic-style torches in the hall — spiral-shaped things holding gilt flame bowls.

"It's people like you he fears, Crumpacker."

The only thing you really know about is slot machines, Tony. And twisting people's necks. Look in your antique Venetian mirror and tell me what you see. Your decorators laugh at you behind your back. They sell you a piece of shit from Sri Lanka and tell you it's sixteenth-century Japanese. You've been had, Tony. The people at Piping Rock sit around the club and crack jokes about you. Their neighbor, the collector of crapola.

At the far end of the hall, a squat figure leapt out, blowpipe raised.

Crumpacker waved his fishing rod, and Nathan lowered his weapon. We went quickly toward him. He had a sprig of ivy behind his ear and looked like a potbellied Pan. His frown indicated that he'd had poor hunting. "I musta looked in twenty rooms. Where's he got Amber, in the fuckin' walls?"

"Baloney is asleep."

"Where?"

"I don't know."

"Then how do you know he's asleep?"

"I was listening in on his dreams."

"You and Dr. Doris." Nathan scowled at me. "You see Celia in the living room? What's she think she's doin'?"

"Playing the game her way, Nathan. I never interfere with Celia."

"These wacky broads. Where's Yvonne?"

"On the trail of someone's perfume."

"We've gotta close ranks."

"We have to open doors. Let's go."

I led the march from room to room, each one filled with decorators' spoils, provenance uncertain. And then, suddenly — a middle-aged man sitting straight up in the sheets, confused, as the three of us raced from the door to his bed, Nathan's blowpipe pointed at his head.

"Don't shoot!" he screamed.

"Crumpacker, question him."

"What is your name?"

"I am Chef Cosmo Dominick Pascolini, at your service."

"How do you prepare stuffed breast of veal?"

"You . . . must use good red wine and . . . and be extravagant with extra-virgin olive oil. Then the key is in the browning, just thirty minutes over a medium flame."

"He's telling the truth."

"It can be served cold or hot."

"That will do." I bent in over Chef Cosmo. He was chewing nervously on the end of a decorative mustache. "Which room is Baloney's?"

"This area is for the kitchen staff. He's in the south wing."

"Take us to his room."

"A person gets lost easily in this house." His pajamas were monogrammed purple silk, I saw Crumpacker frowning at them as Chef Cosmo let the sheet fall away from himself. He wore a musk cologne, spoke with a slight accent, had carefully groomed sideburns and manicured fingernails. If our assault on Fortress Baloney was successful, we'd ask him to cook us roast pheasant with truffle sauce. If not, he'd put us through his Cuisinart.

I pointed at Nathan's bandolier, to which dozens of little darts were attached. "Poisoned. If one of them enters your flesh, you'll think you're a sautéed zucchini. So don't try anything funny."

"Nothing funny. I'm just the cook, I don't get involved in family business." He put on his bedroom slippers and purple robe, and then stood between us. "My sole concern is with how fresh are the funghi."

"He should do a food column," said Nathan, "for *Ladies Own Monthly.*"

"I go to the village for vegetables, I come back to my kitchen. About anything else I'm not informed." He preceded us into the hallway, his footsteps fearful, for he had the prospect of Baloney in front of him and a blowgun behind. "I come from a line of chefs that goes back to the court of Catherine de' Medici. If I should die, many secrets will be lost."

Being with Chef Cosmo was making me feel peckish. Searching my coat I found that Siggy's mother had secreted a blintz in my breast pocket. No sooner was it out than Chef Cosmo turned, nose twitching. Crumpacker poked him with the end of his fish pole, and Cosmo resumed his march, but he kept sneaking glances at me. "Here." I gave the chef the last bite.

He sniffed at it closely. "You found it where?"

"In my breast pocket."

"Who made it?"

"Mrs. Blomberg."

"Ah, Mrs. Blomberg." He nodded, as if understanding, was still sniffing the blintz when we heard a noise ahead of us. Nathan's blowpipe came around to his mouth, and Crumpacker's rod went back. Chef Cosmo pointed his bit of Mrs. Blomberg's blintz toward the hall window, which was going slowly up, lifted by two pudgy pink hands; the arms twisted, an elbow came in, then a leg, then the other leg. A white flash of underpants. "Siggy!"

Siggy lowered himself into the hallway. He was covered with twigs and leaves. Shlomo's trousers were now split completely up the back seam. "I'm lucky I'm friggin' alive. Who's this guy?"

"Chef Cosmo Dominick Pascolini, at your service."

"He's leading us to Baloney."

Siggy fell into step between Nathan and me. "When that vine let go, I thought good night Irene." He picked twigs off his coat. "I got such a zetz in the back from that hedge I fell in."

I turned to Chef Cosmo. "We saw a woman in white."

"She is Princess Camilla of the ancient noble family of Monteforte."

"What is she doing here?"

"She has told me that she's being held here against her will."

"We're going to put an end to it."

We continued forward in a phalanx of war, past a bust of Dante, and then the Four Seasons in marble — little cherubs bearing the buds of spring, the flowers of summer, the fruits of fall, and the rock of winter. And then I had a vision — of a mobster as big as a water buffalo, one for whom the crunch of bone was a musical tone.

"What's up?" Sig, steadying my elbow.

"Nathan, get your blowgun ready."

There were double doors ahead of us, trimmed in gilt and fitted with polished brass handles.

"Chef, you're going to go through those doors, just as though nothing were wrong."

"*Sì, sì,* and then?"

"Nathan, you and Crumpacker flank the door in battle positions. Siggy, what are you doing?"

"I just remembered this pack of crap Madame V gave me. I'm supposed to swallow it, right?"

"At the appropriate moment."

"Somethin' tells me, Howard."

"Now?"

"Or never." Siggy opened the small packet, tapped the contents into his mouth, and chewed thoughtfully. "Halvah it's not." He swallowed, stared at me. His eyes slowly rotated in their sockets. Beads of perspiration broke on his upper lip and his ears turned bright red. "Oy . . . oy . . . oy . . ." His eyes disappeared up into his head.

"Sig, what's happening?"

His mouth fell open. He took a few uncertain steps, like a wind-up toy on its first walk, marched straight into the wall, and turned mechanically around. His eyes rolled back down into view like two lemons on a slot machine, with a kind of click as they settled into place. His body convulsed, a spasm that rippled from head to foot, and then he began to bounce up and down with little bounds, feet together, hands at his side. "Son . . . of . . . a . . . bitch . . ."

"Sig —"

". . . I . . . got . . . a . . . spring . . . in . . . my . . . pekl . . ." He bounced around the hall in the most bizarre fashion, as if an invisible hand were lifting him up and down. ". . . help . . . me . . . Howard. . . . I'm . . . going . . . to . . . bounce . . . out . . . the . . . window . . ."

"What's with him?" asked Nathan.

"He took a powder."

". . . oy . . . oy . . . oy . . . oy . . . oy . . ." He pronounced the syllable on each bounce, just as he lifted off. ". . . my . . . noodle pudding . . . is . . . gonna . . . come . . . up . . ."

"Grab him by the ankles," said Crumpacker.

"We might break the spell."

". . . oy . . . oy . . . oy . . ."

"Well, all he's doing is saying oy."

"It comforts him, Crumpacker, surely you can see that."

". . . they're . . . getting . . . higher . . . the . . . bounces . . . are . . . getting . . . higher . . . Howard . . . I'm . . . goin' . . . through . . . the . . . frig . . . ging . . . roof . . ."

He was deep in the trance now. His voice rose and fell eerily, as if he were bouncing over whole neighborhoods.

I turned back toward the door, and the atmosphere heaved against me again, a thick wave of violence moving heavily along.

". . . oy . . . oy . . . oy . . ." Sig was bouncing toward me, jowls going up and down, eyes gazing in two different directions. I grabbed the double doors and flung them open.

Another endless hall whose only item of furniture was an antique billiard table on which three goombahs were having a late-night game. Startled, they looked up at us, then threw down their cues and reached for their guns, but I already had my own captured pistols out. I pointed and squeezed the triggers, which remained frozen, safeties on. I fumbled with them frantically, but they were stupid hunks of iron in my hands, the sort of pistols one finds in a dream, obstinate, impossible to fire, sworn to obey their true master only.

Siggy came down from his bounce and collapsed, knees buckling, hands dragging the carpet. His head fell into his chest, and he rolled forward, his arms and legs folding inward, compressing him into a ball.

The goombahs fired at him, but he was already rolling along the carpet, muffled little oys emerging from inside the tight little ball he'd become. He picked up speed, his underpants a blur of white as he rolled along with voodoo velocity. The goombahs leapt aside, but Siggy caught them like tenpins, taking the feet out from under them as he rolled on by, disappearing down the long hall.

They tried to get up, their misfired bullets burying in the walls and ceiling. Nathan's cheeks puffed out, and one of the goombahs fell backward, clutching his leg. I brained another with the butt of my pistol, but the third found his footing again, firing with both arms extended just as Crumpacker made a brilliant if fortuitous cast, catching the nearby drapes; he yanked back and the drapes billowed out around the goombah, wrapping him in. He thrashed free, but Nathan got him in the back of the neck with the wrath of the pygmy, the dart burying in just above his inelegantly gaping collar. He sagged to the floor, gun slipping from his paralyzed fingers; he

groped toward it numbly, made a few little pawing motions
on the carpet, and then collapsed in a heap beside his two
colleagues, making three unconscious goombahs in a row.
But I still felt the heavy shadow moving against us in this
house. "Nathan, where's Chef Cosmo?"

"Got away."

"It doesn't matter, Tony Baloney knows we're here now."

We dragged the goombahs into an adjacent room, dumped
them into the closet, and slid a heavy antique bureau in front
of the door. "You guys came through," said Nathan, as we
stepped back into the hall. "I'm goin' to increase employee
benefits for both of you. From here on in, the water cooler's
free."

Our attention was drawn toward the shadowy depths of the
hall, from which the sound of oy came faintly. And then
Siggy stepped into the light, holding his head and shuffling
toward us. He was still bent forward slightly, and his legs
moved in a rubbery manner, toes pointed out. ". . . oy . . .
gevalt . . ."

We hurried up to him. "Sig, are you all right?"

"He asks am I all right." Sig looked at me, his forehead
bruised, his ears still scarlet. The arms of his sport coat had
been torn from their seams. "I get rolled down the hall a
hundred miles an hour and he asks am I all right. I hit that
friggin' wall like a cannonball." Sig put both hands to his
spine and rubbed it tenderly. "Madame V knows how to mix
a powder."

"What's at the end of the hall?"

"I heard the plaster crack as I hit and I'm krechtzing to
myself and tryin' to get up off the floor when I see this lady
in white. She was beautiful, Howard, real class. Then the

whole place starts spinnin' and guns are blastin' and when I came to she was gone. It's the story of my life."

"That was Princess Camilla, Sig. She's a prisoner in this house along with Mitzi and Amber."

"I'll tell you what we do —" Nathan was excited now, punching his freckled fist into his palm. "We take the princess back to her family. They lay a big reward on us and we invest in slum real estate."

Crumpacker looked dubious. "She's not worth a nickel."

Nathan snapped at him. "What do you know about abducted princesses? You're new to the firm."

"Suit yourself," said Crumpacker with a shrug of infinite boredom. What did he know about Princess Camilla? And how had he found it out? I suspected a voodoo vision he'd not informed us of.

I took the lead down the hall. When we passed the spot where Siggy had crashed into the wall, he bent down and picked up a piece of white chiffon. "She was real." He held it to his face and breathed in. "A princess." He pocketed the piece of chiffon and straightened his posture, then marched forward, arms swinging, the white lining of his ripped armpits sticking out in two little points. "I'm comin', Princess. Sig is on the way."

We continued down the adjoining corridor, through the recreational wing of the mansion. We passed a cedar-lined sauna with hot tub and bath, then a video room with a large-screen projection system, where a film was still running, starring Mitzi Mouse. She was in all her feathers, well, actually very few feathers, in fact only the wisp of a feathery smile and a pair of pearl-studded boots.

"The boots are all wrong for her," said Crumpacker.

"Why don't we take five?" said Siggy, sitting down.

"We got no time," said Nathan, yanking him upright.

Siggy's eyes remained on the screen as he backed toward the door. "Do you suppose Baloney makes the princess star in beaver flicks?"

"Royal Princess Pushed Into Porn. Make a note of that for the *Examiner*, Howard."

We stepped back out into the hall. Beside the video parlor was a trophy room, door ajar, its lifelike shadows luring us into its depths. Bright shields and spears decorated the walls. The furniture was made of horn, and the footstools of elephants' feet.

"Should be the head of Big Al Mastachenza up here somewhere," said Siggy, walking along below a wall of stuffed wildebeest, water buffalo, impala. Light in the room was dim, coming from a pair of lamps whose shades were parchment skin, the soft reddish glow causing animated reflections in the glass eyes of the nearby animal heads. Most realistic of all, perhaps, was the glitter in the eyes of the large animal in shadow at the end of the row, rearing on its hind legs, hairy paw reaching out toward Siggy.

A small oy! escaped our ad manager's lips.

Nathan's blowpipe came off his shoulder as Siggy's attacker stepped into the light, clubbed Siggy once on the noggin and dropped him. It was a world-record goombah. Nathan fired. A dart struck the fellow in the cheek and hung there. He smiled at Nathan. "I'm gonna rip off your head and shit down your neck."

Nathan fired again, trying for more sensitive tissue, and struck a direct hit in the fellow's ear lobe. I knew from Dr. Husbands's broad-ranging health column that important bodily meridians met there, and severe disorientation should have ensued by now, but the impervious goombah was laughing, as he grabbed Nathan, cracked his blowpipe in half and then punched our publisher to the floor. Nathan looked to me in desperation.

Crumpacker and I collided with each other trying to get out the door. The huge bear of a man was on us with surprising quickness, had us both by the collar, was about to smash our heads together when a bloodcurdling scream sounded and a whirling black object struck him in the center of the forehead. It quivered there for a moment, its sharp star points gleaming. I turned and saw Hattie Flyer in the doorway, arm still extended, but it had not been enough; the throwing star fell to the floor, rejected by the bony armor of the goombah's oxlike brow.

"Run, Hattie!"

She ran, but the handsome young hoodlum she'd been guarding was directly behind her.

"Hattie," I cried, "you untied him, didn't you?"

"I Wanted To Reform Him," said the foolish woman.

A white-veiled figure appeared at the end of the hall. Princess Camilla's hand went to her mouth, stifling a cry at the sight of us caught in the grip of her captors. And then the goombah holding us in the air completed what he'd begun, which was cracking Crumpacker's head and mine together. In the midst of shooting stars I saw Madame V's face and heard her counsel:

Lizard skin and parrot's tongue . . .

Crumpacker's belt was our only lizard skin and we'd already used it. Parrot's tongue was a mail order item.

"Pair of fuckin' assholes." The giant goombah dropped us

to the floor, where Crumpacker became tangled in his own fishing line. The goombah picked up the pole, looked at it. "What's dis for?"

"Fishing's my hobby."

"Killin' assholes is mine."

He seemed to have that nicely in hand, following which he kicked us in the kidneys, as practice for this year's Olympic Gangland Games, which we'd be covering for *Macho Man* magazine.

"Leave them alone!" screamed Hattie.

"Shut up," snarled her handsome young captor. "Or you'll get the same."

"Just because you're good-looking you think you've got it made," said Hattie. "But in my story you wind up in a trailer park."

She was hysterical, as were we all. Crumpacker looked at me in terror as the goombah continued kicking us across the trophy room toward the door. "Are we going to be murdered?" asked the cardinal.

"I believe that is the intention."

"Who'll take care of my Abyssinians?"

"They'll be found and cared for, old man, beauty always is."

We were yanked to our feet. Hattie clawed and shrieked beside us. "Your Kisses May Be Hot And Wild, But You're Still A Punk!"

"You're a real nut, lady, you know that?"

"I Won't Be Moping Over You, Johnny."

"My name ain't Johnny."

"In my story it is." She gave him a look of such withering intensity that Johnny drew back, his energy field seared by rays such as only a passion-magazine editor could generate, and a sort of fizzing sound came from her lips. Had her saliva been tested at that moment by Dr. Husbands's experimental laboratory, I believe properties dangerous to human life would have been found in it.

Two more guards appeared, dragging Siggy and Nathan from the trophy room. "Easy," said Sig, "I'm a disabled veteran."

Nathan fell against me, holding his head. "They outflanked us, Howard." And then he whispered, *"We're not licked yet."* I sincerely hoped he was right, but as they kicked us down the main staircase toward the living room I saw they also had Fernando trussed on the floor beneath his mural.

"You see what he done to the boss's wall?"

"Tony ain't gonna like it."

They yanked Fernando to his feet. "What's wrong with you, Pancho? You crazy or somethin', writin' on people's walls like that?"

"You give me one more hour, then you see somethings," said Fernando.

Of course *I* could already see the pathologically distorted Paleolithic hindquarters of another Big Womans, but I'd been trained to observe such details.

"Come on, move it."

"I *am* moving it," said Crumpacker, still entangled in bits of his line.

"You went fishin' in the wrong pond, pal." A swift kick to Crumpacker's rear.

"Here now," I protested, "that man's an ordained minister."

Whap, across the side of the head. Amidst shooting stars

and colored wheels I heard Madame Veronique again: *Take the hand of one who has been hanged or strangled, dry it in the sun in the dog days, or if the sun should not be hot enough, dry the hand in the oven.*

Was she out of touch with the situation? "Sig," I whispered, pretending to fall against him, "Madame V says we need a severed hand."

"Tell her we ain't got one."

"Knock it off." *Whap, whap,* a few more clouts to the head. Siggy bounced away from me, elbows up to protect himself. "Gimme a break, I useta live in the neighborhood."

They kicked him a few more times, and herded us into an outer wing of the ground floor, one wall of which was glass bricks, now filtering the gray light of dawn into the house. Through a pair of French doors to the garden I spied the figure of Uqal Mussa creeping across the grounds, the marble nymph on one shoulder and a stuffed pillowcase over the other.

"Shoot that guy!"

Two of our captors rushed out, guns drawn. Uqal Mussa raced toward the wall, threw nymph and pillowcase over, then leapt at the wall himself, scrambling up as bullets careened off it in little white puffs of splintering stone. One could not help but appreciate the grace with which he climbed, body seeming to dodge the bullets by some sixth sense, ancestral no doubt. He paused at the top of the wall, turned to his pursuers and gave them his turn signal, after which he dropped out of sight beyond the grounds. They followed, but had little of his inherited agility. By the time they'd struggled to the top of the wall, I knew that Mussa was long gone, with pillowcase and nymph, tracking along as his forefathers had before him, their blessing upon him, and the loot of the ages over his shoulder.

"Your pal got away," said the goombah guarding me. "Too bad for you." I heard the song of a bird waking outside, its little spirit happily greeting the day as it rose from its nest. Upon a nearby table was a collection of paperweights, and they too were reflecting the first gleams of day, beside the yellow marble bust of a child and a polished wooden box on which an hourglass sat, its white sands still.

One of the thugs reached out and turned the hourglass over, then pointed at it with the muzzle of his pistol. "That's how much time you got," he said with a laugh.

The sands run slowly, said the voice of Madame V. *Trust in the Djab*.

I caught a glimpse of an adjacent study, with freshly cut flowers spreading in a white vase. There was a portrait hanging there, of Grandfather Baloney I believe, in dark suit and darker scowl, gaze protecting the corridor from the likes of us. *Mine,* said Grandfather B, black eyes boring into space, heavy brow permanently creased by struggle in a violent realm. His mouth was implacably set, and yet I saw in the corner of it a little turn of compromise, such as one had to make in business. Give and take, mostly take, but now and then I give over, said the mouth, to keep peace.

We all praying to Djab, said Madame V, and the portrait of Grandfather B seemed to nod in agreement.

"Toss Me Around, You Beast, I'm Just Your Plaything." Hattie was still kicking and hissing bitterly.

"You try to bite me one more time, bitch, and I'll pull your teeth with a pliers."

Hattie straightened herself to her full height and spoke from the pages of her fantasy monthlies, where good men rescue fair maids. "Alongside me is the editor of *Macho Man,* and punks like you are nothing to him."

Macho Man was kicked the full way down to the cellar. As they dragged Hattie off in another direction, I heard her telling them that punishment meant nothing to me, that no amount could ever break me. Feebly I lifted a hand, and was kicked in the wrist, which shattered my watch.

The sands run still more slowly now, said Madame V. *This omen is good.*

I've never been much of one for omens, they always seem so flexible.

Sig and Nathan helped me to my feet. "Don't do anything else to make them mad," whispered Siggy to me urgently.

I propped myself up against him and resisted the temptation to make a premature show of strength; now was not quite the time for Macho Man to reveal his deadly fighting methods. Now he would hold his aching sides together and take a caffeine mint.

We were herded along a basement corridor past the screened-in enclosure of the Baloney wine cellar. Hundreds of bottles rested there in ruby darkness. On the other side of the corridor was a pantry, containing flour barrels, stores of spices, herbs, sacks of beans, and hanging ropes of garlic.

"We're in Chef Cosmo's area, Crumpacker," I whispered. "We may have an ally in him."

"I can't think why," said Crumpacker. "We threatened to shoot him with a poisoned dart."

The goombahs opened another storage chamber; we were herded in, and the door locked behind us. Tins of olive oil lined the floor, along with jars of pimientos, pickles, cans of cured ham.

"I tell you," said Fernando, flopping down on the floor, "I had one hell of a picture started upstairs. A cow, a dress, everything goin' right."

"Rations," said Nathan, prying the lid off a jar of olives. He dipped his hand in and passed the jar around. "We gotta keep our strength up for the next assault."

We shared the tangy black morsels. Then, with my Swiss army knife, which was now coming into its own, I opened a can of ham and sliced off thin strips of the delicious treacle-cured meat. But the atmosphere remained that of men trapped; the storage room was windowless and gloomy, its door thick and heavily guarded.

And then I spotted the air duct overhead — a large tin conduit whose sections were held together by machine bolts. Quickly I opened another blade of my Swiss army knife, revealing a Phillips head screwdriver. "Nathan, Fernando, lift me up."

They did so, and I unscrewed a section of duct. A single tug separated it, and a warm draft of air blew over my face. "One of us has to explore this and see if it leads to the outside."

"A simple recon mission," said Nathan.

"Don't look at me," said Siggy. "I'm not crawlin' into that thing. What if I wind up in the friggin' furnace?"

"It won't be in use at this time of the year."

"I'll roast in there. I got overactive sweat glands. Hey, wait a second . . . goddamnit . . ."

We stuffed him in the duct, not without some difficulty as he fought all the way, but finally we had him wedged in, with only his feet dangling out, and then the worn soles of his shoes disappeared into the darkness. We quickly closed the opened section and replaced the bolts. Faint shuffling sounds echoed along the duct, finally faded.

"That man should be singled out on the parade ground," said Nathan.

"Much as he might appreciate these military honors, Nathan, a raise would be more to the point."

"The men who serve under me aren't in it for the money."

Fernando was studying the wall. "I got room here." He reached in his pocket, brought out his grease pencil.

"How can you think of cows at a time like this?"

"Oh, let him," said Crumpacker. "What possible difference could it make now? So he draws on their walls, big deal. They're going to shoot us anyway, aren't they?" His eyes filled with frustration. "What are my cats going to do without Daddy to look after them, oh these existential dilemmas are so unsettling."

"Don't lose your grip now, old man."

"Why shouldn't I? I've been Mr. Cool for years and where has it gotten me? I'm locked in a storage room with the pickles."

"And very good pickles they are, Crumpacker." I was opening a bottle just then and sought to give him one, but he knocked my hand aside.

"I'm sick of being a reasonable person." He flung his arms wide. "I feel the new me emerging."

"Not here, Crumpacker."

"Yes, right now, right here in the pickle room."

Nathan pulled at my sleeve. "Take it down, Howard, we

can run it in *Prophecy*. Tell us about it, Cardinal. Spill your guts out."

"I'm feeling my feelings at last. I'm having a catharsis." Crumpacker kicked over the empty olive jar and sent it rolling along the floor. "*That's* for all the bullshit I've taken my whole life."

The jar struck the wall and shattered, oozing olive brine. "My whole fucked-up family was dysfunctional. Who kept them all together? Little Forrest, that's who. The perfect little gentleman. Well, I'm sick of it, do you hear me? Sick, sick, sick of being a gentleman!"

"Crumpacker, you'll attract the guards."

"Let them come. Do you think I give a shit?"

Fernando was watching with his mouth hanging slightly open. A cloud seemed to be passing before his eyes, the light dimming within. Slowly his arms raised at the elbow, and a moment later his two fingers were sticking in the air.

"Ease off, Crumpacker, you've precipitated a catatonic seizure."

"Truth is liberating."

"His pulse is slowing."

"From here on in, I'm going to tell people exactly what I think."

"Give me a pickle, Nathan, I'll run it under Fernando's nose."

His arms remained outstretched, his breathing shallow, and his eyes continued to stare blankly at Crumpacker, who was still expressing the New Me.

"I tried to always stay bouncy and bright. Well, horsefeathers on that! Do you hear me? Horsefeathers on it."

"Pushing the boat out a bit far, aren't you, old man?"

"Good old dependable Forrest Crumpacker, take him any-where and watch him behave like David Niven. Well, I've had it. I'm going to tear around and behave like a maniac. Look at him —" He pointed at Fernando, who gazed back blankly. "— he ruins walls, throws fits, acts violent, and no-body cares. They just say, that's how he is, he's a little crazy. How does *he* get away with it and not me? Answer me that. Because he just *does what he feels like*. And he's the heal-thiest person in this room."

"I'd hardly call catatonic rigor a sign of health, Crum-packer."

"Oh, he gets over it fast enough. And then he goes on doing whatever he wants without a thought of what other people will say."

"Crumpacker, we are held prisoner in a gangland cellar with our only hope of escape being Siggy in the air ducts. I'm not trying to dilute the wonder of your psycholog-ical breakthrough, but surely that fact must alter it some-what."

"Let him talk, Howard," said Nathan. "It's a Dr. Doris column if I ever heard one."

"That's right," said Crumpacker. "I'm Dr. Fucking Doris!" Suddenly his raving stopped. "Oh god, what's going to hap-pen to my *plants*?"

"Have a pickle, old man."

He shook his head. "I feel the rage boiling inside me, and all my life I've hidden it behind a wooden mask."

"Your face is remarkably animated, Crumpacker. I'd go so far as to say it's one of the more lively countenances I've encountered."

"Yes, but it's not *mine*. I'm just a puppet, a creation of my family. Did you know my father was a general in the army?"

Nathan snapped to attention. "You carry within you the seed of a proud military tradition."

"I'm lucky I'm not in a mental institution."

Much as Crumpacker's self-development interested me, I was now hearing a sound in the air duct.

". . . oy . . . oy . . . oy . . ."

They hoisted me up, I unloosened the bolts, and opened the duct. Siggy's eyes came out of the darkness, and we helped him down.

"What did you find?"

"I think we can make it. We might come out the chimney."

We turned toward our staff artist, whose fingers remained pointed in the air. "We can't get him in the shaft like that." Nathan went over to him and pushed down on one arm. As soon as he let go, it popped back up. "He'll get jammed, and we'll never be able to budge him."

"So what do we do?"

"He'll be our rearguard action."

"Standing here with his fingers in the air?"

"The element of surprise."

With Crumpacker's help, I struggled up into the duct. My shoulders were wedged painfully, but I managed to crawl forward, and Siggy pushed at my heels. I heard Nathan and Crumpacker behind him as they closed the ductwork up, and then we were in darkness.

By tilting sideways I could just manage to creep forward through the winding metal intestine. Tony Baloney's megalomania had come to our aid. Since even his hot air must flow through ducts bigger than anyone else's, so through them crawled his enemies. Blindly groping, we were once again on the march, and though claustrophobic anxieties swept over me, I called upon the ancestors of Uqal Mussa, those ancient masters of tight tunnels in the houses of the dead.

I hallucinated that I was a corpse in a coffin, a caterpillar in a cocoon, a rat in the wall, until the sound of Siggy behind me quietly groaning oy brought me back to reality. I came to an elbow in the pipe, twisted through, and found myself on a steeper slant, where I had to dig my fingertips into the overlapped pipe joints ahead to pull myself up. The muscles in my arms were trembling, and Siggy hung onto my ankles.

"Siggy, you're pulling me apart."

"Nathan's got hold of *me*."

And Crumpacker had hold of Nathan, and I was pulling them all up through darkness, our wormlike chain of magazine men twisting, grunting, heaving itself along through the bowels of the house. Blue balls of hallucinogenic light swam up before my eyes, drifting by or popping open to reveal scenes from incomprehensible dimensions of voodoo magic. Faint drumming noises sounded in my mind, along with the clucking of chickens.

Then I saw a more mundane glow ahead of me in the duct. I struggled toward it, and found myself peering up through a floor grate at the stockinged legs and lacy underwear of Celia Lyndhurst. I paused before revealing myself, as I was, after all, the editor of *Bottoms*, and the pause proved timely, for a second later the door opened and the lord of the manor, Tony Baloney himself, limped in on his wounded leg — an angry-looking man in his fifties, with a bumper crop of eyebrows and a chin that seemed to have been cleft by an ax. In spite of the early hour, he was studiously groomed in a suit Crumpacker might have approved were he not buried below me in the duct. Celia turned coolly toward Baloney as he bellowed, "Who the hell are you?"

"The question isn't who am I, Mr. Baloney, but what are you doing with that horrible couch in this room?"

His head snapped back like the bull's when the matadora flips the cape that so cruelly deludes him. "That couch belonged to my father!"

"It should've been buried with him. I saw what you *should* have in here last weekend on Madison Avenue. An Empire daybed, really a sleigh bed . . ."

"You're — a decorator?"

"I can see fifteen things, at least, that are completely wrong with this room."

"You can?" The Lord of the Manor, stunned. Celia, with perfect instinct, pressed the attack:

"Those heavy drapes — throw them out."

"Do you know how much those drapes cost?"

"Money, Mr. Baloney, is *hardly* the issue. You want yellow taffeta curtains, yellow produces clear thinking and aids communication. This *is* your office, isn't it? Well, then yellow is essential. Before I studied scuba diving I took a seminar on color therapy and I can tell you that yellow not only relaxes mental tension, it aids in digestion."

Baloney, still reeling: "How do you know about my digestion?"

"Who wouldn't have bad digestion with those drapes? And

that couch, and this *red* armchair, much too much energy for proper assimilation. By the way, who suggested you buy those Dali prints? Don't you know Dali prints are like quicksand real estate in Florida? A bad investment, Mr. Baloney, the market is flooded with counterfeits."

Baloney's expression had darkened to a sort of primal purple, which is not a color everyone can wear. He was taking quick suspicious looks at his couch, his drapes, his Dali prints. The momentum was all Celia's:

"And that *desk*."

Here Baloney smiled, a thin superior smile. "That happens to be a late-seventeenth-century cartonnier."

"Late-nineteenth-century Borax. Gaudy pieces like this were given away as a premium with soap flakes."

He gave a choked little gasp. The matadora had put the sword between his shoulder blades. He reached a hand out toward his precious desk, then wavered, and dropped it to his side.

"Young lady . . ." He looked around the room, from gaudy piece to gaudy piece, distrusting it all. "Why don't you and I take a little walk through my home? I'd like your opinion on certain items. Just between you and me, OK?"

"Mr. Baloney, I'd be only too happy to help you. But first, don't you think we ought to talk about my friends?"

"We'll talk about them after we take our little walk."

"I'm not walking anywhere until I know that my friends are safe."

"We're going to work them over a little."

"Absolutely not."

"Just a few bruises, so they'll remember to knock next time they visit."

"You're lying to me, Mr. Baloney. I can see it in your eyes."

"All right, so I kill one of them."

"Which one?"

"The one they call Macho Man. The boys say he's the leader."

"That's Howard, you can't kill that poor sweet booby."

Dear Celia, sweet Celia, Celia of the kind heart, you've remembered me and I shall never forget you for it. Your editor in chief, hidden in the air duct, has heard the friendship you hold for him, which not even a goombah chieftain can shake.

"Listen, I've gotta kill somebody, because if I don't I look bad. I got friends out here, and if they find out I let some yo-yos bust into my house and just walk away like nothing happened, my credibility suffers."

"Yees . . ." Celia, growing thoughtful, a finger to her cheek. "I do see your point."

She sees his point. I'm glad of that, aren't you, that she is able to examine the situation from all sides?

"But I promise you, miss, it'll be just one close one in the heart, he'll never know what hit him."

I watched Celia's mind working on a deeper level, the level where old friendships are stored, where the many little things we shared together come to bear and tip the scales in my favor. "His apartment will become vacant, won't it."

"Sure, it'll be vacant, you want it? My consigliere makes a phone call, it's yours."

"With no rent raise?"

"Nobody raises the rent on Tony Bulloni, baby."

"Poor Howard, but I suppose it's his karma to end up this

way, isn't it? I mean, there's nothing I can do, is there?"

The door burst open and a guard rushed in. "Excuse me, Don Bulloni. They're gone! They left the spic behind, he's got like two fingers in the air."

"You dumb fuck, who cares where his fingers are? *Where are those people?*"

"Salvatore says he never took his eyes off the door."

"He's always fooling with the maids down there. Those guys forced the lock and walked right past him." Baloney turned to Celia. "Your pals are too smart for their own good." He glared at the guard. "You find them, you kill them."

"The broads too?"

"No exceptions. Next thing I know they'll be coming up behind me with poison darts."

"That's just Nathan," said Celia. "He's harmless."

"I got soldiers who can't get up off the floor. Am I right, Nuncio?"

"Yeah, Frankie's been chewin' on the carpet for like the last hour."

"And Zalepa?"

"Still droolin'."

Baloney looked at Celia. "I will not wind up drooling on my own carpet." He snapped his fingers at Nuncio. "Go find."

Baloney led Celia out of the room, and I crawled through the duct, with Siggy and the others following. Upon reaching a T in the pipes, I took the upward branch, the others struggling after me. Clawing desperately at the joints, we made our way vertically, elbows and knees wedged against the duct. We reached another T and started on past, when I heard a child's voice echoing from nearby, singing a plaintive tune.

"It's Najaf, Sig. We've got to save her. She's our responsibility."

"Are you kidding me? That little nafka is smarter than you'll ever be."

I detoured into the T and stopped beneath the grate from where the singing came. Yes, there she was, drowning in a white garment five sizes too big for her — the veils of Princess Camilla.

Fate had decreed it. We must rescue them both. It was reckless and probably hopeless, but I couldn't keep twisting endlessly around in this air duct. Call it a beau geste, tell me I'm crazy, but I'm coming, Princess, to carry you and little Najaf away.

"Najaf!" I hissed through the grate, fingers entwined through the wide steel mesh. The child came over to me.

"Hey, what you doing in there?"

"Take this knife. See, it has a screwdriver in it? Unscrew the bolts on the grate."

She began clumsily turning the blade, round and round in her tiny hand. "I have wonderful time, stay up all night, how about you?"

I stared at her through the grate as she fumbled and dropped the screwdriver. "Concentrate, Najaf," I said softly. "That's a good girl."

"I sold two VCR and one microwave."

"Turn it slowly . . . that's right . . ."

"I am dressing up in pretty clothes."

The bolts came out, and I pushed the grate loose. A moment later I was standing in the room, and Najaf was showing me the closet, running her hands through flowing costumes. "See? All belong to the princess."

Siggy's head came out of the duct, curls plastered flat to his brow. He lifted himself up, swung his legs free, and stood, unsteadily. Nathan followed, squinting into the light, looking like Badger from *The Wind in the Willows* had Badger been the publisher of *Knockers*. He did several deep knee bends on his short legs, joints cracking, then ran a hand over his shining wet dome. "That was a narrow beachhead, Howard."

"I've absolutely ruined this suit." Crumpacker, of course.

"Really, Crumpacker, you could hardly expect to come out of an air duct looking your best."

"Her perfume," said Siggy, stepping into the closet and lifting a sleeve to his nose. "I'll remember it as long as I live."

"She is terribly beautiful sad princess," said Najaf. "We be her friends, yes?"

Nathan drew me aside. "We're facin' heavy odds. Our only hope is an orderly retreat. One of us has to draw their fire, while the rest of us go down the vine."

"Nathan," I said, "this is a noble thing you're about to do."

"It's all yours, Howard." He clapped me on the shoulder, and a voice inside me said: From ancient times until now, men have been called upon to sacrifice themselves, and their ranks have been divided between the strong and the weak, and I have always fallen in on the side of the latter, but just this once, just for now, I will hurl myself into the teeth of the enemy, and receive the melancholy reward of battle and certain death.

Overcome by emotion, I walked toward the door. It

seemed impossible that I, Howard Halliday Haggerd Halberd Hammertoe Harm Habana Hades Halston Handy Harley Harmon Heman Hence Hardman Hardon, should be about to die for my staff, but I was cranked up on caffeine and voodoo powder. The music of my soundtrack swelled within me. Head up, chest out, shoulders back, I firmly grasped the knob of the door. It opened toward me with a rush, the edge struck me on the bridge of the nose and broke my glasses neatly in half.

"Howard, if you *will* hide behind doors, people are going to run into you."

"Yvonne!"

"Yes, darling, and look who I found." Mitzi and Amber came in behind her.

"They locked us up in a storeroom full of dishes," said Amber. "We could have rotted in there if Yvonne hadn't come along and gotten us out."

"I have to admit I didn't do it all by myself," said Yvonne. "I was helped and guided by someone you *must* meet, he's one of Mother's real finds." Yvonne stepped back into the hall and extended her hand. A young man came through the doorway, dressed in silk trousers and white shirt, the sleeves of which hung in billowing folds. "This is Paulo, he's Tony Baloney's son."

I held a piece of my eyeglasses up and examined young Baloney closely. He couldn't have been more than nineteen, a delicate-looking lad with nothing of his father in him, except for his eyes, but here he differed too, for his gaze was not interrogative and penetrating but poetic and dreamy. "My father intends to kill you all," he said to me.

"We know that. So if you'll please excuse me I'm going to go and draw his fire." I folded the broken half of my glasses and inserted it into my coat pocket.

Young Baloney stepped back and blocked my way to the door. "I want to be a writer," he said quietly.

"You see," said Yvonne. "Isn't he Mother's best find ever?"

"I write the whole day, but it just seems like I'm pretending." He gazed at me with all the naive passion of his nineteen years. "I know I can do it, and it's all I'm fit for. But how do I get some real experience?"

"Howard," said Yvonne. "Do you *understand*?"

Obeah has done its work, praise Djab, said Madame V.

■　■　■

Tony Baloney sat at a long conference table, his consigliere on one side of him, his first lieutenant on the other. We, the staff of Chameleon Publications, sat at the opposite end, including Hip O'Hopp, who'd been found face down in the phlox.

"All right," said Baloney, "Paulo goes to work for you. You publish whatever he writes in exchange for which I let you go and he moves outta here, *taking everything with him*." Baloney looked at his son, who stared down at the table, and wet his lips nervously.

Tony Baloney frowned, glanced at some notes he'd made in front of him, then looked at us. "And his mother gets to see his name in print every month. Is that correct?"

"Correct," said Nathan.

"He'll learn *so* much working for us," said Yvonne.

"So long as he clears outta here." Tony Baloney shifted in

his chair, wincing as he crossed his legs. He glared across the table at Mitzi. "You nearly fixed me for life."

"The gun went off accidentally."

"I'm a big-hearted sonofabitch. Right?" He glowered at Mitzi, then turned toward his son, whose fragile countenance seemed to fill Don Baloney with rage. "I want everything outta here by tomorrow. That means *all* your clothes. Nothing's gonna be left behind in those closets, capeesh?"

"Capeesh," said Paulo, softly.

The elder Baloney turned to Yvonne. "Me and Mrs. B want you to publish our son's picture too. A *nice* picture he had taken when he graduated high school. Nuncio, get that picture."

The bodyguard rose, departed.

"I want to have a stocking stuffer at Christmas, something to send the relatives. Our son, the published writer. Got it?"

"We'll run it nice and big," said Yvonne.

"Don't run anything of him the way he looks now." Baloney threw another contemptuous glance toward Paulo, whose coiffure was a bit flamboyant perhaps; and his eyebrows *had* been plucked, just slightly. But really, what's a little mauve eye shadow between father and son? I drew my chair forward slightly, leaned toward our host. "Your son surely has the right to be photographed the way he wants, Mr. Baloney."

"Who says so?"

"No one, actually." I slid my chair back.

"I wanna see my son looking like he really is. *My* son. Not somebody else. Not *him*." He hooked his thumb toward Paulo Baloney. "Not somebody Aunt Carmen and Uncle Donato won't recognize."

A butler entered, and placed a large tray before us, on which assorted pastries and rolls were displayed. I hungrily picked one off and attacked it, realizing only as I began chewing that it was a blintz, and not just any blintz, but a Mrs. Blomberg blintz. Chef Cosmo had worked through the dawn to reconstruct a perfect likeness.

Tony Baloney was looking at each of us, his gaze traveling slowly around the table. "Any questions about this deal?"

"We'll be running features by your son every week in the *Midnight Examiner*," said Hip O'Hopp.

"And one of them is about the Bulloni family charities," said the consigliere. "Correct?"

"You've got it."

"And one is about the smear campaign this fine family has suffered in papers such as the *Daily News*."

"We'll correct that erroneous impression, of course," I said.

"Other items will be given to you from time to time as it suits the family."

"Always happy to receive fresh news."

The consigliere smiled and turned to Tony Baloney. "I think we all understand each other, Don Bulloni."

"What is a crusading publication like the *Midnight Examiner*," said Hip, "if it can't print both sides of a story?"

At which moment, Baloney's wife, Margo, entered, golden hair piled high on her head, voluptuous body erect, her forehead and the corners of her eyes wrinkleless, her neck and chin free of any little turkey wattles one might have expected from someone her age. As editor at large for *Ladies Own Monthly*, I felt that in Margo Baloney we had an example of what good diet and a life of complete idleness can do for a woman. Or as Yvonne, seated beside me, whispered in Paulo's ear, "Darling, *who* is her surgeon?"

For her part, Mrs. Baloney's gaze was on Celia, and a gaze of withering malice it was, directed at this chippy who'd attempted to take over the arrangement of interiors at the house of Baloney. Have I mentioned? Celia's reign had been brief, ending when Mrs. B came downstairs for breakfast and discovered her husband being led around the house. She'd gone into action with primal instinct, delivering a speech such as only an ex-showgirl in jeopardy can, claws unsheathed, fangs gleaming. The don's digestion had never been all that perfect, as we know, owing to the little morsels of his enemy's gnawed bones that sometimes caused him mild heartburn; under his wife's assault, he'd imbibed a pint of Maalox. Not for nothing had she worn a leopard-skin G-string at the Copa. And so Celia was deposed, and now sat with the rest of us at the conference table. When her eyes met mine, I only smiled benignly, no hard feelings for that momentary weakness when she'd acquiesced about my getting a close one in the heart and her getting my apartment. We all have our moral limits, and good living space in Manhattan is rare.

Mrs. Baloney walked in back of her son's chair. He smiled up at her and she ran her long red fingernails through his hair. His hand came on top of hers and they exchanged a glance filled with meaning. He was moving out into the world at last, and a piece of her was going with him. "You'll take good care of little Paulo," she said to me quietly, bending down beside me with the freshly dermabrazed skin of her cheek near mine, and I realized — here was the woman for whom I created *Ladies Own Monthly* each month, this was she — a woman completely out of step with the New Age, a throwback, a mastodon, whose cherished ceramic frog at this very moment was squatting by the guest room sink, soap pad in its mouth. I felt a keen emotion, and I vowed that she would remain in my mind's eye each day as I put her magazine together. "Perhaps we can have lunch someday," I murmured. "I'd love to," she answered, and then drew away with studied showgirl elegance. She moved behind her husband, her hand gliding lightly across his shoulder as she passed.

He looked up at her, nodded, and covered a dyspeptic little belch with the back of his hand. He turned to me. "All right, one more thing. Three of my men are missing — Angelo, Joey, and Goozi. You know who I'm talking about? They came by your office?"

Belong to the Djab now, honey, said Madame V.

"I'm afraid that might be a bit of a problem, Mr. Baloney. You see, sometimes in the flow of events there are those who take the path less trodden."

Baloney stared at me, his dark eyes trying to take full measure of this Macho Man with nose-bandaged glasses before him, whose staff had beaten up his dog, written on his living room wall, and stolen his goombahs. "All right, I'm not gonna push it." His eyes closed to a narrow slit. "The dice came up for you." He turned to his lieutenant. "Get them outta here."

Nathan lifted a finger. "Listen, Mr. Baloney, we got a problem down at the office. It could put me right out of business, in which case we couldn't publish your son's work, and he'd have to move back here with his entire wardrobe."

Baloney looked at his son, winced, and turned back toward Nathan. "What's your problem?"

"We got this lawyer after us with a twenty-million-dollar suit."

"What's his name and where's he at?"

Nathan handed him a recent piece of correspondence from the law firm that was pursuing us. Baloney glanced at it and handed it to his lieutenant. "Lean on them."

The lieutenant nodded and Baloney glowered back at Nathan. "Anything else?"

Siggy edged forward. "Well, Mr. Baloney, we got a very high overhead and there's lots of people don't pay their bills. I got right here —" Siggy took a sheaf of papers from his pocket, and started laying them down on the table, one by one. "Imitation Bone China Crucifix with Removable Saviour . . . Genuine Simulated Diamonds . . . Elegant Toupee Center . . . Budget Bust Builder. Can you give me somebody to run these four-flushers down?"

Baloney laid a hand gently on his lieutenant's cuff. "Give 'em No Brains Bennie." The lieutenant nodded and our meeting was concluded. We all stood, and I noted how Hattie Flyer gravitated toward the young lieutenant. I took hold of the cuff of her L. L. Bean marching shorts. "He's Not For You, Believe Me."

"He Slapped Me Around, How Can I Still Love Him?"

"Because he has dark curly hair."

"Howard, I noticed you and Mrs. Baloney —"

"There goes Fernando toward the wall!" I stopped him before he could lay a stroke on the pristine white expanse of the conference room. "Put your charcoal away, and round up your chickens."

I turned to find Hip O'Hopp by my side. "Howard, few

people have ever walked away from this room with a treaty like the one we got." His bloodshot eyes were smiling, scales of pessimism and gloom having fallen from them somewhere in the night. He was staring soberly down the mahogany mile of gangland conference room table. "I couldn't have gotten here as a *New York Times* man. I couldn't have seen this deal go down. It had to be as editor of the *Midnight Examiner*. Howard, maybe we've got a great paper after all."

"Hip, I never had any doubts."

■　■　■

Fernando stood in the middle of my living room, brush in hand, gazing up at the wall.

"She's done," he said.

"Yes, she's marvelous." My bags were packed, of course, along with a few sticks of furniture. Most of what I'd collected over the years wouldn't fit in the new one-room cellar apartment I'd been forced to buy in Hell's Kitchen, but I considered myself lucky to get it at only $175,000. The real estate agent had assured me that the welfare hotel alongside it would eventually be gentrified, and that I shouldn't be too concerned about the murders committed there nightly, because, being in the basement without any windows I was not likely to see them.

"She's my Big Womans," said Fernando, folding his ladder now for the last time, and gathering up his tubes of paint. The doorbell began to ring in one long piercing buzz, by which I knew Uqal Mussa was waiting to take me away.

"Too bad you got to move, kid," said Fernando.

"Yes, well it was that or go insane, I'm sure you understand."

"Is hard to live with great art when it first come up." He

gestured toward the Big Womans. "Fifty years from now she be in all the schoolbooks."

I hadn't been able to paint over her. It was not mine to do. "I'll leave you alone with her now, Fernando. If the landlord comes by, give him the keys."

"Okeydokey, kid. I thank you for the chance you give me to show my stuff."

"By the way, the walls at my new place are much too low for a mural. In fact, I have to go around in a permanent crouch."

"I work any size."

"Yes, but as there are no closets the walls are going to be covered entirely by hooks on which my clothes will hang."

"I figure something out."

I left, toward the service of Aswan Limo, waiting below.

■ ■ ■

The landlord at my old place sued me for property damage; something in the paint Fernando used caused it to keep burning through every attempt to cover over the Big Womans. The new tenants discovered one morning, much to their surprise, that a horrendous monster was manifesting on their living room wall. In three days, she was almost like new again. Ultimately the wall itself had to be destroyed, so the damage suit was considerable, but I called Margo Baloney, and No Brains Bennie paid a visit to my landlord, after which I received a nice note of apology.

So now I'm in my new apartment, and as there isn't space in it for more than one person at a time, I entertain guests at the falafel restaurant above. On the evening of which I now speak, Amber was seated across from me over coffee. "I might have married you," she said, "for just one moment."

"When was that, dear?"

"When you were hit with the door and your glasses broke."

"Never marry for pity."

"No, it was something else. I don't know exactly. You looked so startled, and I seemed to see the real you under all your eccentricities."

"A moment that quickly passed?"

"It was lovely while it lasted."

Yes, Amber darling, and now we are who we are again, and my glasses are in place upon my nose, the better to see how beautiful you are, and how impossibly distant from me in all your chic. The fact I saved your life does not weigh in the scales of your heart, and I quite understand. In any case, I'm having lunch with Margo Baloney tomorrow at the Four Seasons. She likes to meet me there.

"Oh Howard," sighed Amber, "if only you were socially respectable."

We gazed at each other over the candle flame. Her green eyes, so expertly made-up, looked into mine. I took her hand and squeezed it gently, glancing around as always to see if anyone in the restaurant needed a Heimlich maneuver.

■   ■   ■

After putting her in a taxi, I wandered through Hell's Kitchen and into Times Square, where I saw a familiar face — Mitzi Mouse looking at me from a twenty-five-foot-high poster advertising her latest — *Hot Honeys Kinky Fetish*. Her eyes followed me seductively but I knew her mind was on the French rondeau.

I continued on downtown, and found myself in the Village at evening's end, walking along Eighth Street through the bright bazaar of beads and rings, designer shoes and electric dreams. It was crowded as always, and I felt as if I were visiting it in my sleep, something that happens to New Yorkers after a number of years, we drift out of the material environment and live instead on its vapors, like lotus-eaters, poised slightly above the blossom, which is neon red and green.

I walked past the carnival, to that desolate block made up of corrugated sliding doors. It's the spiritual dividing line between east and west, and just after it is Astor Place, with its eternally lonely island floating in traffic. Standing on that woeful spot, held there as are the souls in Dante, was a man selling candy-covered apples, which no one bought, perhaps because he also wore a sign on his chest which announced that

HE THAT DIGGETH A PIT SHALL FALL INTO IT

His eyes were glazed, as were his apples, and he was babbling to unseen figures in the square, ghosts and genies he alone perceived. Something in his figure drew me near enough to see — it was Angelo the suave and handsome goombah whom Madame Veronique had turned loose without a calabash, and here he was, holding an apple on a stick.

I purchased one, it was the least I could do.

"The End Is Near," he said, handing it to me.

"The End Has Come," I said, and walked on.